A MESSAGE FOR MR. LAZARUS

A MESSAGE FOR MR. LAZARUS

BARBARA LAMBERT

A NOVELLA & SEVEN STORIES

The publisher gratefully acknowledges the support of the Canada Council for the Arts and the Ontario Arts Council for its publishing program. We acknowledge the financial support of the Government of Canada through the Book Publishing Industry Development Program (BPIDP) for our publishing activities.

THE CANADA COUNCIL | LE CONSEIL DES ARTS
FOR THE ARTS | DU CANADA
SINCE 1957 | DEPUIS 1957

The following stories from the collection have been published previously: "A Message for Mr. Lazarus", "The Queen of Saxony" and "In the Blue House" in *The Malahat Review;* "Where the Bodies are Kept" in *The Malahat Review* and *The Journey Prize Anthology;* "Do You Really Love Me?" in the Canadian Fiction Magazine anthology, *Carrying the Fire.*

Printed and bound in Canada.

Canadian Cataloguing in Publication Data
Lambert, Barbara Rose
A message for Mr. Lazarus : a novella and stories
ISBN 1-896951-22-8
I. Title.
PS8573.A3849M48 2000   C813'.54   C99-901527-3
PR9199.3.L35M48 2000

CORMORANT BOOKS INC.
RR 1, Dunvegan, Ontario K0C 1J0

For Douglas,
who makes everything possible

CONTENTS

AN INCIDENT

I will not tell you his name because he was my neighbour. If his wife were to learn that I saw him last week in Port Alberni, she would surely be confused. He died two months ago.

We had stopped at Fryer John's for fish and chips, on our way home from a vacation at Long Beach. I had ordered oysters. "How many oysters in a serving?" I had asked the waitress. "Twelve," she had replied. A dozen oysters. Heaven. It was moments later that J (although he has been my love for many years I will call him J, because of an unexplained sadness he carries, which I know he would not like me to explore) pointed out our neighbour at a nearby table. Our neighbour had ordered oysters too.

Not surprisingly, the man was alone. Our neighbour had always had a quiet (almost affrontingly quiet) manner. Self-contained, but sending out tendrils of sensitivity which sometimes, briefly, I had imagined waving in the air between us like a challenge, so prickled, so contentedly sure of being misunderstood — sly, I had perhaps unfairly thought, for when these tendrils retracted I had felt clumsy, every time. Long ago, at a neighbourhood party, he had kissed a woman, quickly, in the kitchen. When he let her go, she had felt clumsy too.

In the café, he read his newspaper until his order arrived. He kept the paper neatly folded into thirds, to the right of his knife and fork. There was none of the usual irritating rustle and bungle when he unfolded and refolded to read another page. It was clear that here was a man who would not get newsprint on his fingers; no need to fear for his pale-grey and camel clothes. When his lunch arrived he ate with an appreciation revealed only by a certain shine on his gold-rimmed glasses, the attentive tilt of his straight, blameless, banker's nose.

You mourn for people, of course. When they die suddenly, long before they are supposed to, you understand their children's horrid sense of deprivation, the anger of their wives. Yet it was only when I saw our neighbour in the café in Port Alberni, that for a moment I thought I understood something of the shifting boundaries of loss. I recalled a day, about a year earlier, when he and I had stopped and talked together for a few minutes on the street. His wife was at their holiday place in the Interior for the summer. He was only semi-retired, so he joined her every other weekend, something like that. He was coming from the store; he had bought the right ingredients for a meal of his own invention, involving carrots, celery, wieners, all sliced diagonally. He seemed happy about this. He seemed to be a slightly different person than I had ever talked to before. I asked him how his semi-retirement was going. He told me he had started writing a novel, *The Boy in the Woodshed*. He said that this boy, who grew up in a small town in the Okanagan, used to escape the turmoil and unhappiness of his family by going out to the shed behind the house to write poetry.

Our neighbour would go moody for no reason, his wife had often told me. He would stop talking for days. "Why don't you scream?" I asked her once. "How can you stand it? Why don't you rage, and tear the house apart?" A ridiculous concept, of course; she is a woman whose house glows even in the dark, a cool white neon cleanliness. "I'm not allowed to lose my temper" was all she said.

For years I had felt my neighbour was a man whose very essence spun out a fussy strictness. Never mind if that was just a defence, when his wife was so bound up in those strands. Even I, occasionally, had felt a need to be on guard. When I stood talking with him on the street, last year, I could not help remembering one hot night in summer long ago, when he had phoned to tell me that it was ten o'clock. "How" (he had reasonably asked, his voice a thin white thread) "can I expect my wife to get my children to go to sleep, when yours are running around outside?" "Oh *thank you*," I had replied. "Thank you so much, for letting me know what time it is." After that, it is possible that we did not speak for several years.

My oysters were not very good. Perhaps that is true of twelve of anything.

Our neighbour ate all his lunch, however, all his chips and coleslaw too. He never glanced our way. Just as well. I wanted to ask about his writing, but I know how annoying that can be. I wanted to tell him that even if he never got around to finishing his book, I would remember the boy in the shed and how he wrote poetry.

"Strange," I said to J, between frizzled bites that exploded into greenness, scalding my tongue, "to imagine that the dead might turn up in other cities, completely oblivious of the sadness back home. Do you think they would want to know that they are missed? Or would they rather just be left alone?"

My dear love did not answer. Instead, he raised his dark hurt eyes to mine. He said, "I see my father, many times."

"You see your father?"

I felt the tingling caution of a hunter. I knew I was approaching something fleet and rare.

"I saw my father just last week, downtown. He was walking up the street right ahead of me. But then he turned to go into the bank," J said, "so I carried on to the University Club."

IN THE BLUE HOUSE

When my sister was in London, two years ago, she bought me a Liberty wool shawl. She has given me so many lovely things over the years, and I always end up having — very tactfully — to give them back to her.

"Now, it's just a little thing," Lolly said when she got back to Vancouver that time, as she reached into her big Italian bag. I was pouring her some apple-cinnamon tea. We were sitting by the picture window, which Mick had criss-crossed with strips of lattice to give the look of diamond panes. Two chairs carved out of barrels painted black (with bright red cushions) faced one another there, across a glass-topped cable-spool. The apartment was full of all that Mick had done for me, in fact. The bathroom lined with cedar shingles was another fine example. *The old farm privy turned inside out?* I remember kicking myself for thinking, when he surprised me with that on my return from work one day. And of course now Lolly was looking around morosely at all this evidence of Mickey, shaking her head at how I'd thrown away a perfectly good man. This was before I had the least idea that I'd be living in the blue house in a few months' time.

My family has always known what is right for me. *He's just an Irish charmer, it won't last, he's too good to be true* — that was the verdict on Mickey at the start. When I'd settled down with him, and gone back to study something practical, *Maybe she's finally found herself this time* was what flashed back and forth in hopeful code. By then, even if they'd heard what Mick said behind their backs, they would merely have put it down to his lively tongue. "The Universal Pundit," Mick called Geoffrey, when Geoff kept popping up on TV about the fate of the nation. "Cheese it, the Pundit!" he'd say and switch the dial, or else sit forward in his chair, pulling a long face like a camel, mimicking Geoffrey's tone.

Lolly had asked the people at Liberty's to wrap the shawl in that famous peacock pattern, and I couldn't help a flutter underneath my breastbone. *She has brought me back some wonderful thing.* At the time I was filled with a vast and indefinable need, a situation that had been getting worse and worse. My sister travels all around the world with her husband, as he chairs conferences and accepts honorary degrees. "Yes, Geoffrey has been invited to Stockholm," she will say (or Rome, or Israel), "and he's asked me to go along." Then she'll laugh, shrug — throw up her hands. "I was so sick that whole week in London," she was explaining as I unfolded the square of paisley wool, "that going to Liberty's was more or less the most exciting thing I did. We went to the opera, and my ears were so plugged I could hardly hear a thing. And then one morning I went out and I saw this, and I immediately thought of you."

That's what happens, every time. I ask her over so I can hear about her trip and she gets shifty. *It's so ghastly being sick away from home, but I thought of you.*

After I moved to the blue house, I liked to imagine how any day I would step across the inch-wide chasm separating me from the person I needed to be. I had planned to get back to doing portraits right after Mick finally agreed to leave. At one time I'd earned good money doing charcoal drawings at festivals and fairs. I'd persuaded Mickey to take away the trestle table and all the chairs he'd built, so that I could turn that cramped apartment into a proper studio. I had cut back my physio practice from three days a week to two.

Please don't think I was looking for another man when I untangled myself from Mickey. Oh, I can't deny I'd had clichéed glimpses of myself — candlelight dinners, say, on the tightrope between acquaintance and desire. *Would you like some black pepper?* (Time and again that waiter on his unicycle zooming in to steal the scene, but still I'd be lit by roving searchlights, way up there.) I had pictured going out dancing, too. Mickey never wanted to go out dancing; I moved around too much, he said. That was so depressing, considering how he used to follow me from town to town, in my professional dancing days.

"Or let's just say, back when you got paid to take your clothes off," my sister would bite her tongue to keep from remarking, if I complained. Lolly is a conundrum to me, not in what she says, but in what she doesn't. She's sloshing around inside with opinions she keeps the lid on, a situation which I believe could have helped to change her very shape. She used to be beautiful once. I used to look up to her in everything. It scares me that she's become almost as big around as our mother's old wringer washer (though the silky, tweedy clothes from Holt's help her put on a good show), and even when she's trying hard to be supportive, she can't help that kind of completely flattening smile. Back when I quit art school to dance in bars, "Hey, as long as you earn a living" was the most she'd ever bring herself to say. "It's nothing to me if you've got all that talent and don't use it — and it's too late to shock Mum and Dad." No use explaining that it was the dance itself: the movement and the costumes — the sequined five-inch heels, the feather boas — that made me feel alive in those days, and not the eyes of all those men.

What a surprise, after Mickey, to find that I had turned invisible. *Maybe you smile too much,* my sister said. *They're running scared these days.* The vertical lines above her mouth pursed when she said this. Would that be my mouth in ten years?

I suppose it had made Mickey proud but edgy, the way other men looked at me. I am six feet tall, and in those days I wore my hair in a wild shelf of curls, which I was managing to keep the same colour as when I was known as the Pink Lady, the big sensation at Number Five Orange, and so on. I moved with a dancer's grace, still, as well. And though I was sometimes forced to watch myself devour a dozen Chinese pastries in a row, and follow that with a carton of ice cream — though I had to confess to the horror that this occasionally happened — mostly I kept myself on a careful rein. The caution came from Mummy, I guess. *You could be very pretty, dear, if you just entertained a little discipline.* That hunger got worse, not better, after Mick left. There were times when I was so ravenous I could have eaten up the world. Some patient lying on my table would find me gazing at his toes. And my sister's prescription for this was another dose of discipline. Even my plan to move to the blue house she saw as retrograde. "Just when I've got you the commission to do Mary Bramwell's portrait! " she told me in a shocked voice on the phone. We talk several times a day, for some reason. "And that place is falling apart, you know."

I'd had my eye on the blue house for years. It's jammed between a warehouse and a used-furniture store just east of Main — high and narrow, with gingerbreaded eaves — one of those originals that date back to the turn of the last century, now weathered to that lovely shade the Munchkins wore in *The Wizard of Oz*. The owners have a chocolate factory in the basement. They are a stubborn old couple, friends of parents of friends. He makes the mixtures; she spends the days trapped inside a circular counter, so crippled with arthritis that she can hardly move, dipping the shapes by hand or ladling bittersweet fluid into moulds.

They have been doing this all their married lives. How do people get into such a box? I think of my mother and my father, all the years ploughed into rows of vegetables so someone else could gather up the dreams. Such a hard example set, so many encouraging words. *You have great natural talent, dear — but you will have to work at it, you know...!* I have never understood the inner mechanism — mine — that made those words a trap and not a spring.

Lying in my bedroom in the blue house, I could tell the day of the week without ever going outside. Monday, chocolate-covered cherries. Through the narrow space between my window and the warehouse drifted the smell of boiling cherry liqueur. Tuesday was the day of the truffled mice — trays and trays of upturned little creatures, some dark, some light, their stomachs turning shiny in the breath of the fan. Wednesday the delicious smell of roasting pecans woke me up. Praline day. Thursday was for soft centres, Friday for hard. Far into the night, I breathed in the precarious smell of caramel brought to precisely two hundred and ninety-five degrees.

Why couldn't I nourish myself just on the smells? Why did I have to crave love or food or any other thing? How was it that the outline of myself could all at once dissolve, when I least expected it, into an ocean of need?

That shawl Lolly brought from London was red and pink and orange, with flashes of a peculiar glassy blue. "Kaleidoscope colours!" she cried. "Doesn't it take you back to your child-hood, Zee?"

It made me feel restless, right away. It made me feel stub-born, and somehow bad. Also I couldn't help picturing her walking the streets of London — London! where I might never be able to afford to go again — along the crescents of white houses, in the soft April rain. Day after day she passed shops filled with rarities from the far-flung corners of the world, knowing that I, her only sister, needed some small and talis-manic detail that would pull me back into view — the right pair of earrings, the essential perfume. And then she dashed into Liberty's and came out with a woolly piece of cloth in the colours our mother would have worn.

"Oh my, it's so beautiful," I heard myself exclaim, "but I don't think it goes with a single thing I own. Here, let me hold it up to *you*."

Some months later, however, when it had become clear that things weren't opening up the way they should, I saw that I was absolutely and completely and forever through with making everyone feel better but me. I would chuck my exact-ing job. I would go to London myself, take hold of every-thing I'd missed the first time around. No shops for me — just brilliant people, visits to galleries, exposure to new ideas.

And when I came home, I would plunge headlong into supporting myself as an artist. Sink or swim.

Before I left, my sister gave me seven stretchy garments — mix-and-match — all in shades of beige and puce and soupy green. That was very sweet of her. There is no point feeling insulted when someone repeatedly gets you completely wrong.

Why was I nervous when I set off? I'd hitchhiked all around Europe when I was eighteen. My poor parents had sacrificed enormously to send me to the Slade, and I never could explain why the approach of that school was stifling to me — why I took off and spent that entire year wandering, *hooking up with some really beautiful people,* as I told them in my letters, believing they should see how that made the whole thing worthwhile. Do I wish I hadn't done that? That Christmas with Dieter, for example, in his cold-water basement flat, hardly a civil word between us, making love to keep warm? Even from this distance it looks better than being somewhere else, tied down.

The portrait Lolly had persuaded her friend Mary Bramwell to have painted was to be a birthday surprise for Mary's husband, one of the top dental surgeons in the city. If this went well, I might be commissioned to do the whole Bramwell family. "If you can do this, you're in," my sister said. "You'll be doing the whole town before you know." Mary Bramwell was on the board of the opera, and of the symphony.

Immediately on my return from London — rather like an omen — the sculptor who'd had the two top floors of the blue house was finally evicted for months of unpaid rent, leaving an unholy mess behind, but also a north-facing skylight in what had been the attic, a rough space obviously destined to become my studio.

My cat wound himself around my ankles as I spackled and painted the rooms down below, glad to be sharing my life again after my sister's stringent care. Together we pictured how the light would filter kindly into that high-ceilinged place up there; how the Bramwells, one after another, would sit in my afghan-covered chair; how, when my charcoal stroked the paper, they would gladly offer up their likenesses.

Lolly believes doing a portrait is much like what she does at the Craft Museum, when she draws up a docent file. You put one line on the paper, and then another and another, and you get them in the right place and, before you know it, you have a copy of a person looking out at you. She believes I am over-particular, as well. We have been through this many times. *Oh but that is like him,* she'll say. *Please don't go niggling and niggling away at it. That woman has invested a lot of energy bringing her little boy to come and sit for you. Don't disappoint her by saying you aren't satisfied and you'll give her the thing for free! Come on — you're in the smoke-and-mirrors business now.* Still, she had confidence I could do the Bramwells because I'd started going over to a place called Rat's to sketch the neighbourhood kids who hung out there after school. Those kids could look tough, but their quirky faces jumped onto the page. I let them keep the sketches, in return for posing. No obligation, just a lovely exchange. And in that noisy smoky place where every second word was *fuck*, I saw how wrong my sister was: how capturing a likeness is neither discipline nor smoke and mirrors, how it is a gift, but not a gift that I or any other person can possess, how the act of giving passes back and forth, on a clear stream of love.

"I see that cat-litter box is still there," my sister said, nodding at the battered yellow plastic container at the end of the hall. "Interesting visual effect." *Considering how much time you've spent on everything else down here,* she wanted to say. This was not about the cat box. This was about Mary Bramwell, and how, instead of pulling the studio into shape, I was concentrating on my living space on the lower floor — Lolly failing to grasp, as so often, the importance of the wholeness of things. But she would rather plunge her hand in boiling soup than come right out and tell you what she means.

"Don't you have a *scarf*?" she said next. I'd been wondering out loud if I'd be okay going out in my trench without a sweater, not having a full-length military swagger coat like hers, talk about visual effects. *(Crikey, if it isn't the Michelin man on the retreat from Moscow* had been rattling through my brain as I followed her upstairs. Sometimes I do miss Mickey a lot, it's true.) Then I had to confess — on the subject of scarves — "Oh, Jan and Mickey gave me a beautiful one for my birthday; Jan knitted it herself, but foolishly I left it on the bus. And I had to give the one Rosie gave me for Christmas back to her. It looked much better on her than me." There was a silence after this, Lolly looking through her purse for her keys, a little too long. "I probably should have kept that lovely Liberty shawl you gave me," I offered.

"Yes," Lolly said.

But that's the most I ever can expect. One day we had a disagreement about our parents' old property out in the Fraser Valley, which we lease for barely enough to pay the taxes. I forget how this led up to what I said — but all of a sudden she sat down on the floor with her head between her knees. "What?" I said. "*Tell* me. Look, just because I mention that you go to all those places and stay in the best hotels, when the most I can manage is three weeks in London at the Y, it doesn't mean I want a life like yours — in fact I've gone out of my way *not* to have a life like yours. All I was doing was opening up my heart to you." She was breathing so hard I thought she was going to explode. Then she jumped up and ran into the kitchen and dumped half a bottle of sudsy ammonia in the sink and started scrubbing all the cupboards, opening and slamming the doors; and after that she got going on the floors, boring into the corners, scraping at the built-up wax with one of my good table knives. "Christ," she was saying, "Christ, Christ, Christ — bloody hell!"

Jan was wonderful for Mickey. A pediatric nurse, and bright as a button — a button of steel, I almost said — small and blonde and shiny, and she kept everything pulled together. By the time I got back from my trip, she had Mickey working full-time for a computer firm, and they'd bought a house and taken on a mortgage.

My sister liked to think it meant something that he kept

coming back to visit me. She had never understood how I had been stuck in my life with him, not able to give him what he needed, not able to leave — not able to allow him to touch me, finally — and him being so good about it, saying, *Darlin' it hardly matters, the whole business is highly over-rated anyway*, and then lying on the couch reading Kafka day after day. "Look," Lolly kept saying in those days, "there's no such thing as a perfect man. He doesn't make you suffer enough, that's his problem. Well, count your blessings." Something crossed her face and maybe I should have pursued it, but that's not the way we do things. "Stop expecting the impossible from him. Naturally he doesn't want to go dancing when you're making those moves all over the floor. Get him to *work*, Zee. If the two of you worked full-time, you'd be able to travel all around the world, you know."

Last fall Lolly brought me back perfume from Rome.

How is it possible, from all the sexy shops along the Via Veneto, that my sister could choose something that — when it settled down — smelled like the oil you put on to keep insects away?

As I stripped the walls of my new home, room by room, ragged glimpses of past lives presented themselves to me. Patches of forget-me-not curled away beneath my knife, and looping garlands, and sunbonnet girls in pinafores. And I scraped deeper, peeled and tore.

The clinic had been glad to have me back. I had no choice but to go. Once again those broken people stretched out upon my table. Sometimes I looked down at my hands and they were hammers. Where could this possibly lead?

But if you can do this, you're in. Yes, the day finally came when I could no longer put off the portrait of my sister's wealthy friend, though my studio was still nothing but a skylight and a dream. It is one thing to have your subject come to you, quite another to creep into someone else's territory with all your awkward gear.

The Bramwell house was set far back on a lawn, and the lawn rose in smooth-mown terraces. I remembered rolling down lawns like that when I was a child. I considered doing it now. Hello, I would say, when she came to the door — I hope you don't mind, I'm just having a bit of a roll.

I heard the yapping of a dog.

The dog was white, the carpet was white, the woman was blonde and dressed in cream. She planned to pose by the unlit fire in a white leather chair. The room was cold, and the light was terrible.

Mickey and Jan gave me dishtowels for Christmas this year, twenty of them, brilliant orange, with a red lacquer basket to keep them in. "Well, we didn't know what else," Jan said. "We didn't want to make another mistake about something to wear." Last year they gave me a yellow angora sweater but it made me sneeze. For my birthday they brought me silver earrings from Beckwoman's, chunks of turquoise bound in heavy silver wire, which unfortunately pulled my ears down and made the pierced holes ragged and long.

Twenty towels in screaming orange. I had spent weeks painting my kitchen in subtle shades of acacia, picking the mouldings out in toasty cinnamon. But I did not have the heart to return this gift of glaring waffle-weave. Into the trunk at the foot of my bed it had to go.

That trunk was a box of guilt I'd lugged around, a carbuncle on my soul. Over the years it had filled up with objects too particular to give away: the copper charm bracelet my mother and father brought me back from their only trip to Mexico; the school ring of the first boy I ever necked with; a book of the wisdom of Kahlil Gibran, a gift from an aunt when I got my physio degree. Why did these sad harmless objects piss me off? They seemed like pieces of myself locked in there — hands, wrists, ankles, eyes — bronzed reminders of some person I had miraculously escaped being.

"Perhaps you should have a long-range plan," Lolly had taken to saying, in that tentative way — the way my mother used to speak to me too, as if I had to be treated with kid gloves, as if I alone carried the fragile vessel of my mother's hopes.

A plan, for once a plan. Such a flat word. Plan.

Going to London had been a plan. I didn't even want to think about that now — how in London I had wandered the streets, the whole thing spoiled by a kind of jealous gluttony. Other people had that city every day. In those panicked hours of walking, I could not make it belong to me in any way. Perhaps there was nothing for me anywhere, in any corner of the world.

The entrance to my studio was through a trap door in my bedroom ceiling, and I had closed it off recently. A year before, I had started keeping a book of dreams. Now I saw that over and over I had emerged into wakefulness held by the tentacles of plants, the sticky petals of flowers. When I thought back and tried to picture those forms, they were awful; but in my sleep I was filled with a sensation sweeter than love or food or anything I'd known.

My bed was a mattress on the carpet, beneath that closed trap door. I had left this room for the last, understanding that everything must be exact in this chamber. I had finally painted it the colour of the inside of a seashell. Even in half-light the room was filled with a rosy glow. A private colour, a secret colour, the colour flesh turns when it gleams above the rising tide that sweeps every other thought away.

"And how many times did you repaint it, before you got to that?" My sister, of course.

"What you have to understand, Lolly, is that I'm an artist. You know how I am."

A sharp in-draw of breath at the other end of the line.

It had not been easy for Lolly, the business with Mary Bramwell. When, after four or five sessions, Mary and I mutually decided that the portrait was not going to work out — when she did not even accept the sketches I tried to give her — Mary Bramwell went out and bought her husband a Rolex for his birthday instead. *Think of that, Zee. That's how much she was prepared to pay.*

A Rolex. A gleam of gold, and a face full of dials, and a

bracelet that expands. I wanted to discount everything that stood for. Instead I imagined the mottled moist metallic-smelling wrist hairs underneath the band. The touch of some unknown hand. In a moment, in the dark, the way the blind read — this would discover exactly who I was, translate me back into myself again.

Mickey was waiting in my kitchen when I came home from work two days ago, with a determined devil-may-care smile, and a bottle of wine. He grabbed my arm and propelled me down the hall. "See, I've made your bed and now you'll have to lie in it," he said. "Hey don't get me wrong — that was just a play on words." He didn't understand my look at all. "It's a copy of an early Canadian sleigh bed," he was saying. "It took me months just to find the proper wood, you know." I tried to find one single thing to say. An oblong box with two massive chunks of cedar, head and foot, bulging up and then curving under, like the ends of violins — the whole thing finished in dark bubbled varnish, the wood below rough-hewn, making me think of those statues of bears you see in parks. For a moment I imagined it was a joke, or some comment on our years together. *I've made your bed, and now you'll have to lie in it.*

"Now that I'm at Com-Pro I don't have time to do the finish work I used to," he said.

He had dragged this hulk, in pieces, up three flights of stairs. I saw how the years of my life had spiralled down into his kindness, his need for comfort and for praise.

After sleeping in the same room with that bed, I had to call in sick and cancel all my patients yesterday. The thing had skidded around the corners of my dreams all night long, dragging me with it, down spiral staircases and cliffsides, and narrow twisting roads.

But just before waking, I'd had another of those sweet and sticky dreams. I had found a cover to spread over the lumpy ugly beast, and somehow, by wrapping myself in the peculiar texture of the cloth, which set my teeth on edge, but pleasurably — the millions of bristly velvet feet inching across my skin, charging me up with an exorcising power — I was able to ward off the invasion I had been subjected to for years: the constant flood into my life of the most presumptuous, totally unwanted personal things.

Why do people do that? I found myself demanding when I woke. *Why do people get it in their heads that they know exactly what I need? They are deciding who I am. And they always get it wrong.*

Silly to phone my sister and inform her of my sudden plan. "You should try the white sales, then," Lolly said, "if you are determined to lose your job just to find the right cover for your bed." Whatever she truly thought or didn't think — about my dreams, my drifting life, or any other thing — submerged, as always, in that half tact of hers, followed by the need to organize. She put the phone down before I could protest, and fetched some flyer from a linen shop in Metro-Town, and read me the prices of sheets and towels and duvet covers. "We could meet and have lunch there," she said, "after I've taken Geoff's mother to the dentist and then dropped her back at Sunny View — oh, and I have to pick up Geoffrey's book from the printer — but maybe tea then, and I could drive you home." It's sad, really, the way she allows all these errands to gobble up her time.

But she should be more careful, I was thinking as I hurried to the SkyTrain. The very thought of ploughing through the sales laid me low. By then, I had no idea where I was headed. All I knew was that something deep was going on. I changed to the sea bus and rode across the harbour, and caught another bus to West Vancouver, and changed again and rode along Marine.

It was one of those grey January days, the trough of the year. Why not keep right on going, hop a ferry, sail to the Island? A feeling came over me that I remembered from childhood, of how the world is curved — a curved grey surface skidding off to the horizon, with nothing to hold you but an effort of will. To stop that queasiness, I started trying to picture one single place where I wanted to be. I saw myself arriving in some up-island community, by bus — checking into one of those hotels I used to know so well. I walk into the bar. Every head turns my way. An expectant hush. I have no choice. Slinky move by slinky move, I bring the Pink Lady back to life, and the place goes wild.

But even if it doesn't, it wouldn't be the end of the world. I had to smile, thinking of that continuing curve of ocean, islands, further continents.

Yet all at once I was tugging the cord, I was charging down the aisle. The bus slid to a stop in the middle of the street. I dashed for the sidewalk through the slush, just missing being hit by a car.

In the window of a shop that sold oriental rugs, draped over a black lacquer screen, was a fall of lush brocaded silk. This was what had caught my eye, just a flash of iridescence through the grey winter day, like the folding and unfolding of a wing. And the cloth still seemed to move. The pattern changed colour, shifted, gleamed, as I walked back and forth on the sidewalk. Improbable leaves and flowers caught light from one direction, then another; and peculiar shapes, either butterflies or fans, flickered the way the sea does, first water, then fire, before the sinking of the sun.

"It is a very fine example of what are known as Bizarre Silks," the owner said. His voice also had a soft brocaded sound. "This piece was woven in France, perhaps at the end of the last century — look, here in the selvage is the symbol of the Brothers Goncourt. But these designs, my lady" — he lowered his voice, widened his eyes — "were patterns that filtered from the Orient at least a century before, inspired, I am afraid to say, by hashish dreams."

Why had I taken the bus in that direction? Why had I found myself there? Why was the cloth, when it was measured, the exact amount I would need?

"But this price is only for today. Indeed, you will have to make up your mind before my wife comes. She will never agree."

"Seven hundred dollars!" My sister's voice bumped the phone

right off my ear, when I called her in the evening.

"I took my share of the clinic rent," I said calmly, though I felt higher than I'd felt for years. "Look, Lolly — my life is about to change. I can't go on with that work any more. Trust me for once. I know what I'm doing."

I didn't even try to tell her the rest — how when I held that fabric to my skin the sap began to flow. How I knew that if I slept beneath those watery gleaming shades they would surely, sooner or later, lure love into my room.

This morning I had to call in sick once again. That ruinous fabric was not what I had thought. It was much darker than I'd thought. Last night, even when I brought in a standing lamp, those strange ambiguous shapes absorbed light and absorbed, sucked away the rosy glow. I had made a terrible mistake. I had traded what amounted to my future for someone else's hashish dream.

"Zee, come on, relax," my sister said, predictably. "The clinic will just have to wait for the rent. And after a day or two you'll decide that fabric is absolutely fine."

"No!" I could feel a hot wire of stubbornness down my spine. "I had to lock it away in my box. If you want to buy it from me, fine. Otherwise that's where it stays. It's not right, and I can't have it around where I have to look at it even one minute more."

"Oh, Jesus bloody Christ! You spent seven hundred dollars on it yesterday and now you've decided you can't look at it any more?"

"Don't use that tone as if I'm crazy."

"Oh, hey, sorry. Let's not say crazy, let's say sick. You are just unbelievably picky, Zee!"

Why did I hold still for that? There was something in her voice I'd never heard before. I felt a nasty swoop, a thrill. I had to poke around, see what more she might reveal.

"I suppose now you're going to start in about all the gifts you've given me."

Her silence rushed down the line, and I could see her with her head between her knees, trying to keep from saying all the things she wanted to. For once I got it wrong. "You are abso-bloody-*lutely* right. Now that you mention it, it is incredibly demeaning the way you do that — as if the things people knock themselves out to choose are not just wrong, but an insult in some way! As if, as if.... Oh bloody hell...!" I could hear her voice slide away from the phone.

"Lolly! Don't you dare fade away on me right now. Don't go and start fucking cleaning things."

"No such luck. I'm going to tell you how you've always pissed me off, okay? You want everything, but nothing is ever good enough for you — no gift that anyone gives you, and no man who ever loves you, and worst of all, nothing that you yourself ever do! And I'm sick of it, and I'm sick of hearing about it. And if you don't get that seven-hundred-dollar piece of flim-flam out of the box and back onto your bed, I will never talk to you again. I've had it, Zee."

So I am lying beneath it now. The room is submerged in the greying afternoon, but I have wrapped myself in the wavering shapes the sun must make as it penetrates the caverns of the sea. I float in the calm after the storm. Flotsam is everywhere. The place is strewn with all the things I pulled out of the box — the silver hoops that used to turn my ears green, and the pearls with a rhinestone clasp, and the wooden beads and the glass beads, and the pink carnival bear. The Mexican bracelet sways in the window, its copper charms chiming as it turns; and hankies lie around the bed, like fans of lacy coral — and books of verse with gilded spines too beautiful to crack, and diaries never written in, and a pen with a nib too fine.

A bittersweet smell drifts into my room. A scene from my life rises up before me — this scene, but as it would appear if I were the famous illustrator of books my mother used to believe I would become. Look, here is the old dwelling on the cover, tall and quaint, allowing views into all the rooms. A nest of long-legged birds tilts at an angle on the roof. Bright flowers trail from the sills. Details, details — I bring them all into being. Children hang out the windows of the apartment down below, breathing in the chocolate fumes, or lowering themselves towards the basement window on trellis vines. They peer and point at that old couple, bent and industrious as gnomes, who refuse to give up, who pour all their conscious days into the same tight mould, the hard miracle of constancy. This is a book of riddles, I see. High above, in a rose-hued room, a woman has come to rest among shapes that can fill or empty, like the moon.

WHERE THE BODIES ARE KEPT

I don't have a lot I want to think about just now. The job is finished, the order has gone off by Federal Express, the house is silent as the grave. Truly, the phrase describes the state I fall into at those times when one thing is finished and I have no idea what the next thing is going to be. This is the break I've been longing for, for weeks. Without a moment for relaxation, decomposition begins.

So I turn my mind to Kate Rutherford instead. Thank god for neighbours, I say — thank god for Kate at least, pretty Kate — for her glorious imprudence, which I can take a good close look at when my own life does that trick of dissolving and filling up my lungs with dread. Kate lives just up the street on the edge of Lighthouse Park, in a noted West Vancouver house, five levels of glass and stone. It was about three years ago that she smashed her husband's BMW into a hydro pole with such force that, among other things, the whole neighbourhood had to do without power over the crucial dinner hour. How many candle-lit romances did she spark, I wonder — how many families talked and listened in the flickering strangeness of their suddenly cavelike homes?

Some weeks later, Kate made it home from the hospital, in a taxi, alone.

I imagine how that was — how she stood in the hall of that great glass house where the inside merged with the outside, the dripping cedars all around, the glass roof streaming with rain. I picture her tugging at a strand of hair, pulling that curl until she could chew the end of it, tasting the familiar sliding crunch as the hair dampened and went limp between her teeth.

I listen — not to the rattle of a shingle on my own roof, but to how that house of Kate's must have echoed as she stood there in the hall.

She was staring at a tall Italian table that held a vase of flowers, five purple irises, a few narcissus, a large white lily — all a few days old. Beside the vase was a note, on a sheet from one of Charlie's prescription pads. "I've sent the children out to my sister in the Valley," she read, "until you decide to get your feet back on the ground. I won't be home for dinner by the way — late surgery."

No slam-bang arrival then, to wait for — three teenagers bursting in the door, dumping down their bags, carping at one another, scattering their coats and shoes; not embarrassed by her presence, no! Just glad, relieved, *obviously* glad to have her home.

I feel the closing in, the chill: how that glass-roofed hallway shrank down to something smaller than a block of ice, how she hung suspended in the cube of silence, like a speck, *until you decide to get your feet back on the ground.*

Dreamlike, it would feel, to be so frozen — and then a sudden thaw, a rush of vindication, as she went over to the mirror, checked the face that had been miraculously spared, remembered how she'd trembled when she made it up an hour before, taking care to do it all the way he liked it: mascara but not eyeliner, shadow of the most delicate bruised blue.

She snatched her purse from the chair by the door and rifled through her wallet. It was too late for the bank. Anyway, Charlie had closed their joint account some time ago. Still, she had enough for a day or so. She could hear the taxi tearing up pebbles down near the street, as if the driver had run into some sort of trouble in the dark and the rain. So she ran after him — slipping on the gravel, ripping her stocking, bloodying her knee, muddying her camel coat horribly. She hammered on the hood just as the car was creeping out into the road. As she settled into the back once more, she caught the driver's eye in the mirror. She saw the way he was reassessing her. She said to herself, Well, what do I care?

She tried to make him race along Marine Drive. The road twisted past houses like her own braced on the cliffside, also English-looking timbered and leaded manors, and the charming seaside cottages where bankers and stockbrokers had retired to grow roses and putter around. She hurried him across Lion's Gate Bridge, and through the darkening park, to Vancouver proper. "Take me to the West End," she told him, then. "Oh, I don't know — just anywhere."

All of this happened before I knew Kate, before I suffered the enormous change in my own life that caused me to move here, to this part of West Vancouver whimsically known as Tiddly Cove.

I bought a house at the crossroads of The Glen and The Glen. One of those streets is actually The Glen Wynde, but as everyone who needs to know this is presumed to know already, the signpost doesn't bother to explain. This struck me as a good-natured omen when I first viewed the house. You could hardly get lost, could you, if no matter which way you went you were still on the street that led you home?

Tiddly Cove. It is a metaphor of course, though the streets are right there on the map. It is the invention of cartoonists, who have made it the epitome of what eastern journalists like to refer to as Lotus Land. And why not, I said, the morning after I arrived. Let them call it anything they want, the poor buggers, still up to their ankles in snow. I jogged along The Glen, following glimpses of the sea. The air was full of robins, and the squeaks and peeps of a hundred other birds, the rush of wings. Bluebells bordered the road on one side, and red-leafed masses of false geranium in tiny pinkish flower. On the other side I was passing a heavily wooded area, huge alders, the trunks spattered with a brilliant greenish crust of lichen. Then the woods gave way to the small harbour — a sailboat bobbing at its buoy, a beached canoe — and sunlight played upon the rocks, the driftwood, the water, and the scent of broom tangled up the air.

There was a grassy nubbled park a little farther along the road — one remaining apple tree (that morning in full bloom) from what had once been a seaside orchard. The dewy meadow flashed with a scattering of small reflected fires. I sat on a rock, in the sun. Across the street, and all the way up the hill, the gabled, shingled houses peered through their pocketing of trees and shrubs and flowers. How could it be possible that anyone — *anyone* — (of course I was thinking of myself) would not be happy here?

I design fabric for a living, *Surface decoration — you might try a bit of that yourself,* the aunt who raised me used to say. That was in the days when she still dreamed I might improve my looks, no matter what, and pick off a doctor or a lawyer. The way Kate Rutherford nailed Charlie, long before he even got to med school, would have struck Aunt Jackie as masterful.

Yes, I deal entirely in surface. I would love to go deeper, believe me. I would love to illuminate the ticking of the clockwork of the universe, I would love to be able to make clear, in the curve of a woman's cheek, or the lines of a rock or the whiteness of a flower, how everything relates to every other thing. Also I'd love to have an artist's verve, the audacity of Attila Lukacs or Picasso, or the nerve to wrap the Reichstag, the confidence that rests on supreme technical control. But the fact is that I embarked on the creative life without a scrap of talent. I have the eye, and I have the horrid burning itch — also the bottomless pit that I sometimes think might be filled up by recognition — but I still can't draw a line.

Perhaps that's why I have always had such a peculiar fellow-feeling for Kate Rutherford. Even the first time I met her I couldn't help a shiver of recognition. My moving truck had just driven away; I was surrounded by crates, upturned chairs, baskets crammed with earrings, socks and undies, also all the paraphernalia of my craft, which I was going to have to fit into a house far more cramped and decrepit than I had fondly thought when I closed the deal. And now this woman was advancing through my gate. A little out of focus, she seemed to me, but I was tired. Her face put me in mind of a shade plant, some determined wavering flower.

Yet there was something formidable here as well. That crisp white dress, those brown-and-white shoes with nail-hole patterning, that creamy English-looking skin against the sprightly blue-black curls. A well-kept woman in her forties. *Well-kept.* I found myself pondering that phrase. She was starting up my stairs, frowning in a way that made me think I'd transgressed some quaint neighbourhood decree. She tut-tutted at the broken tread, lowered herself into the shredding wicker sofa the previous owner had left on my porch (was I catching whiffs of a fruity perfume, or was that brandy?), crossed her lovely legs, unaware that the tops of her knee-high nylons showed, and — turning on me violet eyes set oddly wide apart — said, in a tone of perfect ladyhood which all the same acknowledged how this was wonderfully absurd, "I thought perhaps you'd like to pour me a cup of tea."

Later, of course, various neighbours told me all about the leap to freedom she had taken, a year or so before.

Kate kept the taxi driver cruising up and down the West End streets. It was an adventure for him, she could see. "If you get me through this, I'll buy you a drink," she said, "except — oh shame! — come to think of it, I don't actually drink any more."

"No problem," he replied. Perhaps his religion did not permit him to drink anyway. His dark silky eyes still studied her. His fine brown hands were lazy and adept on the wheel. He understood her kind exactly — *This rich woman,* his expression said, *one of those pretty bitches who pour on the charm if they don't know you, especially if they don't know you, as long as it stays that way* — and Kate saw how he knew full well that when she had found a place to spend the night he would not be invited in; she would not unwind his turban, all those yards of crinkled folds; she would not wrap it around and around her and do a dance for him; and he (appalled, intrigued, against his will), well, he would not *be* there, that was all, for even in imagination she got stymied. A silly phrase came into her head, and tears came to her eyes. *"We're going to have to liberate that naughty girl in you."* That was Fred, the therapist. A lovely man, the one bright light of her hospital stay, the way he had sat and looked at her, with his bulging beautiful green eyes.

The West End, where tall buildings shouldered one another, filled with cubicles of light, filled with breath and life and anonymity. At last Kate saw a promising for-rent sign — an old house jammed tight among the high-rises; a third-floor walk-up, a one-room studio. The driver turned off the meter while she settled the details of the rent, while she wrote out a cheque that would bounce, but she'd deal with that when she had to. The driver's name was Sanjit, and he did not think she should leave her husband. He said *for gratis*, as he put it, he would drive her home right now. All the same, he took her over to Canadian Tire so she could buy a cheap electric kettle and a mug and a roll of foam. "Though I certainly intend to have a proper bed," she told him as he helped her up with the awkward roll, "still the foam will be useful when the children want to have friends sleep over, don't you think?"

"You intend to bring your little children here?"

"They're not so little. But yes, of course."

He gave her his card. "Better tonight you think it over. Any time you call, I'll take you home."

She made a list in her head, that first night, as she tossed and turned. Ikea, yes. She'd make do with the simplest things, for a while. She charted a course for the next day: Duthie's, Ikea, Safeway — the necessary triangle of books and furnishings and food. She pictured this from every angle (a geometric figure that always skirted the liquor store), set it upright, laid planks of demanding simple work across the apex. She would give Charlie quite a surprise with the things she might do.

Next morning she went through the ads. *Home Sewers Wanted* was one she finally had to tick. But come along, Kate, she told herself — here you are, with the one chance of your life to do all the things you've always wanted to do. Last night you went on and on about how you used to have a way with words. Last night, as I recall, you were going to write a mystery.

All night, or so it seemed — flat on her back because of her injured ribs — she had watched a fan of light quivering across her ceiling, which brightened, dimmed, for no reason she could see. Shadows brushed across it, the branches of some sparse city tree. All night she had contained the fact of where she was within the skin of fantasy. She must have read a thousand mysteries these last few years while she waited for Charlie to come home, and hadn't she always said she could do better? Some people made good money doing that.

I can see her exactly, the way she sits up in bed when that thought comes to her. The bare floor, the single thermal blanket, the snippy up-tilt of her chin. "Well, Kate, you will jolly well write one too!" The tone of her father, the brigadier general, later an inspector of schools.

⊖≡⊷ ⊖≡⊷

So, on the day that this is really all about, Kate has been living in that apartment for a year and a month. She has not had a drink in that whole time. And when she looks back at the desert she has crossed, she wonders at the fact that she has made it. *Be patient, Katie. You'll be a different person in a year.* The words of the lovely green-eyed Fred. After she left the hospital she saw him once a week for a while. He gave her courage for a while.

Today, though, she is impatient with herself. She is stepping off a bus at the corner of Hastings and Columbia, in the meanest section of the east end of town. She is facing an unaccustomed challenge, true, but this nervousness is quite absurd. She knows that her mother, were her mother alive, would tell her to buck up. Of course, her mother would also tell her to get the hell out of here immediately and go home.

After she left Charlie she took on a job doing piecework sewing for a jam factory on the edge of Chinatown, in an area of strip clubs and by-the-hour hotels. Her usual routine is to come across town by bus and pick up a week's worth of sewing and hurry straight home to the West End. She does the sewing in the small and dreadful hours, when in any case a deep ache keeps her sleepless. Her children are still out in the Valley. Charlie has threatened to get a restraining order if she takes the Greyhound out there again and tries to pick them up after school; and in fact they hardly want to see her anyway. They loved her all the time she was in trouble, but now that she has changed they allow themselves to feel the shame. Soon though — oh soon! — they will all be singing a different tune, Charlie too.

Normally she would never traipse along this street. But today she is on a mission. The detective book, which she barely dared to dream of a year ago, has moved into the realm of hard research. Charlie would be amazed at how disciplined she has been. She has never once gone out in the morning, as she would have loved to, and walked down to Starbucks for a coffee, then on to English Bay. Instead she has sat herself firmly down at the kitchen table, and filled pages and pages with notes and plans and sketches — and further notes: technical and scientific and forensic, garnered during long conversations on the phone — until her life on the phone has come to be the total of her life.

Fortunately it turns out that she is very good on the phone. She has been amazed at how much information is accessible that way, thanks to just the right blend of practicality, cheekiness, charm. There are men all over the city who love it when she calls, even the way she tells them off if they're too fast, too dry, not clear. It's fun for them, being the expert on the phone, in their offices. Maybe they have paunches, zits, eleven children; she'll never know.

She does not go out in the evenings either, except to AA. And last night she quit that. It's been a year. How much public bloodletting can anyone need?

Kate pauses at the curb, makes sure her handbag is safely slung across her shoulder underneath her fringed cashmere shawl, feels for the notebook inside. She has an appointment with a Detective Sergeant Smeeth — whose job, astoundingly, seems to be not much more than briefing filmmakers and writers. When she finally got him on the line, Kate made some little jest about this, something about how nice it was that for once public money was being spent on *imaginary* crime — the sort of remark her father might have made with heavy irony, though of course Kate meant it strictly in a lighthearted way. His voice was dry and resistant to her whimsy. He did not, he said, discuss any sort of crime on the phone. She would have to come down to his office at the station, then he would see what he could do. It made her think of walnuts, that voice — of how you can stick a knife blade into the crack and sometimes pry apart the shell. Before she left her apartment she took off a floppy hat, and put it on, and took it off again.

This street is truly creepy. It is full of eyes, even though no one looks at her. Kate is wearing a tartan dress with twenty jet buttons, high boots with chunky heels, that cashmere shawl, her bracelet of gold charms. Her parents began the bracelet the year she was born. At school she wore it even for badminton and cheerleading and algebra exams. She makes sure the bracelet is safely tucked within her sleeve.

This is a chill March afternoon. Gusts of cloud, needles of sun. In front of the Brandiz Hotel a man in a plaid shirt and baseball cap is hosing down the sidewalk, and water is spraying up the front of his jeans, soaking his shoes. Kate edges by, carefully, and then skirts the pub of the Roosevelt, next door, which shares an entrance with a steam room and a video arcade. She takes out her notebook...*shares an entrance with a steam room and a video arcade*. A bottle crashes from a window across the street.

"Looking for a place to stay?"

She whirls around. The man who has come up beside her has faded blue eyes with a pinkish overlay.

"Because this isn't where you should look — it's all cockroach heaven along here. This is the most dangerous strip in North America," he says.

Do I look like a candidate for cockroach heaven, she

demands, in a silent voice that is well intentioned, even amused, though edged with a chill that could set anyone back on his heels. *Wobbly poached eyes,* she notes in her head. Still, if the point of this foray is to soak in real street atmosphere, shouldn't she buy this man a coffee? She almost laughs, because isn't this the perfect chance to work at regaining the skill of interacting, as Fred the therapist was constantly urging before she canned him? *Katie, I've never met anyone who smiles so much, and holds herself so closed...!* The man is keeping step beside her. "Go on across Main a block or two," he's insisting. "But along this strip, forget it! Believe me, I should know." He is unzipping the front of his windbreaker, which is made of some sort of silver stuff. He is flapping it open, drawing her attention to a badge sewn on the front. "Look at this — this is Guardia Civil." He fingers a fuzzy oval about the size of a mango, with Chinese letters sewn in black. "This is the official uniform." He stares at her hard, trying to make sure she understands. "Fuck it, you wouldn't believe the fucking stories I could tell you — those bastards have got their grips on every country, it's a fucking scandal. But listen, the minute we get word from Barcelona, we're moving in."

What does it mean when the crazies seek you out to pass on their secrets? Kate gets a most peculiar feeling walking alongside this man, as if she can hear the clicking of the atoms of a parallel universe, every planet whirling in its groove, music revealed to very few.

She gives her head a shake, wobbling her curls. Now she's passing a bunch of men standing around the stairs to the urinal by the Carnegie Centre, and she dodges across the street though the light has turned red, and hurries east along Main, checking her reflection in the windows of the BFK Novelty Shop, the Golden Harvest Cinema, the Needle Exchange.

She is a good twenty minutes early. She sits down on a bus stop bench to pull herself together. She jumps to her feet again; a man is lying underneath. He takes a slug from a bottle in a paper bag, and then rolls over, his face squashed into the shoulder of the curb.

And Kate smells Charlie, suddenly. The way her cheek would come to rest above his armpit, the way she would breathe security from that dank hollow; the way his breath would turn sharp, metallic, after he'd taken her briskly in the dark.

All the choices she has made this past year are ridiculous, she sees. She is exactly the person she was before, only she has spent almost four hundred nights without any human being touching her. All her stupid pride, all that pretending she's about to do some great redeeming thing — what a hoax. She stands outside the Sunshine Café, picking at her cuticles, gnawing at a strip that's torn away, and she sees herself crawling back, flattening right out on the floor. *Step on me. Please.*

Detective Sergeant Smeeth's office is windowless and filled with metal, the chairs and desk and carpet done in shades of handcuff grey. John Smeeth. Call me John. She is dismayed at her own lack of inventiveness, for she would never have dreamed up such a man, yet he is absolutely right: waxy-faced and crafty, a man who understands exactly how the cogs fit the wheels. He crosses the room with a limp, but he looks pumped up with fitness, in a subterranean way. Those murky eyes, those arms as thick as firehoses, very rubbery and pale. He offers to take Kate's wrap. He blinks and then recovers as her bracelet clatters against the metal of her chair. He is doing a complete inventory too, as if all her parts were on a tray for him to memorize — for official purposes, that's the most generous construction.

He settles back behind the desk. "So where exactly does this murder take place?" He removes a cigarette from a pack of unfiltered Players, taps it, stretches back in his chair with his hands folded across his stomach, the unlit cigarette poking out between his balled-up fingers, just below the belt.

If he lights that, I am going to object, Kate is thinking. Though perhaps it would be better lit than where it is.

She catches herself digging both hands into her hair, giving clumps of it a pull. Then she laughs, spreads her hands. "I guess I'm a little nervous. My murder? In fact not far from here."

"A Chinatown murder. Good."

"Well, not exactly. I'm thinking of an old building over on Powell. I work in a jam factory over there — just down from the strip club on the corner. Number Five Orange, I mean."

Just down from the strip club on the corner. She didn't have to say that.

He raises an eyebrow. "So you must work for the famous Jenny. Quite a well-known Chinatown figure, Jenny. Fire department, health department, you name it — they've all had sample cases of Jenny's Jams. Of course that can't have anything to do with the fact the building's up to be condemned."

Kate has to laugh. The way she was brought up, it is absolutely fundamental to laugh whenever a laugh is called for. "You're not saying Jenny's trying to buy city hall with preserves?"

Smeeth's lower eyelids pull up like the rims of a bird's eyes, shoring in dark distasteful knowledge of the way things really are. "So what do *you* find to do in that sticky place, Ms. Rutherford?" He is studying her hands, the bitten cuticles, the fingers scored with sewing-needle marks, maybe even the absence of a ring. "Hey, I have it. Jenny dresses up her jam jars, doesn't she? And you're the one who sews those little apron things. I've always wondered who they got to do that sort of work."

"Well, in fact — "

"And you plan your murders while you sew. I bet you're writing your boss in as the corpse."

"Oh, heavens — I'm just borrowing her premises, you might say."

"Come on, I know how you writers always get the last word in. She has you on piecework, right? Which works out to about fifty cents an hour. You're not trying to support the kids on that, I hope."

"*Kids?* Perish the thought."

Of course that is not what she means. But now, because it came out like a disavowal, Charlie's voice barges in. *"Perish the thought, indeed. There is no judge in the country who would let you within a mile of those kids! What if they'd been in the car? The fact that so far you have managed not to murder any of my children is a fucking miracle!"*

And Smeeth is also looking stern. "But you do have three of the little nippers? Correct?" He reaches over and barely touches her charm bracelet. His stubby finger has a moon-shaped bruise beneath the nail.

Oh you big fat ass, she wants to say, *leave my children out of this.* But she has to fight the urge to get down on her knees. Everything about this stern grey room prompts abasement. *Do you know how thin a baby's skull is?* she could say. *Anything could happen — bricks could fall out of the sky. And that fear goes on and on for years. Do you have any idea what that fear can do to you?* That is the sort of thing she used to say to Fred the therapist, and he would blink his lovely puzzled eyes.

"I see an itty-bitty cradle," Smeeth is saying, the back of a finger grazing the charms, "...and here's a pair of booties...and here's a christening mug engraved with...." He peers closer. "Kyle?"

"Is this a lesson in detection?" Kate keeps the smile in her voice, but pulls her arm away. She doesn't catch his reply, for now it is Kyle's voice she hears. *Please, Mum, please, please, please — we don't want to lose all respect for you...!*

Kyle. Her sweet oldest boy, having to say that on behalf of his brother and his sister. And he is doing what now, because of her? Turning to dope because of her? Listening to music that rots his soul? Charlie will never know what's going on — look how he never had the faintest clue what was going on inside of her. What *was* going on inside of her?

Maybe Smeeth reads some of what she's thinking. "Kids!" he says. "Boy! Hostages to fortune, eh?" She sees that he too has a groove on his finger where a ring used to be. Then he settles back with that cigarette balled up in his fingers again. "So, Ms. Rutherford — confess. I'd say you're just doing that jam job to collect atmosphere."

"Well you'd jolly well be wrong."

He widens his eyes, tilts his head. He shows a gap between his front teeth when he smiles. "No Mr. Rutherford?"

"*Doctor* Rutherford, please.

"No Doctor Rutherford, then?"

"Not since he pushed me down the stairs."

She can't imagine why she said that. She has never mentioned that to anyone. The fact that she dashed out immediately after and smashed Charlie's car up cancelled it out. But if she had to think about it, which she doesn't, it would still be the thing that fills her most with a peculiar feeling she can hardly get a handle on. No, not anger. No, no, no — her therapist was completely wrong — not even shame. When Fred finally pried the story out of her, he said, "Katie, come on — it's absolutely standard for the victim to blot out something like that because of shame." Fred. She loved him so much by then she could not bear to embarrass him by pointing out how he was wrong, how the moment Charlie pushed her down the stairs had been the most thrilling moment of her life, in a way. Thinking of that, she starts picking at her cuticle again.

"Hey, say no more," Smeeth is saying. "So the doctor disappears, so what else is new? I forgot — you're in the murder business."

"Then you're not going to read me my rights?"

"On Dr. Rutherford you get a freebie," Smeeth says.

Oh he's quick, this detective. Kate had forgotten the pure pleasure of words flicked back and forth, but all this is coming back to her, the way at moments like this you can achieve an almost Zen-like rightness. Of course the man is way beyond the pale, as her father used to say. That short-sleeved shirt, the undershirt showing through. The shirt is pushed out flat and hard. What's underneath must be rocklike. "Marmoreal" is the word that comes to her, what a fine sinister word. Smeeth's chunky arms are hairless, white as marble. His chest must be too. You could roll out a piecrust on that chest.

"Let me get this straight," Smeeth is saying. "We've got this dead lady floating in a vat of blackberry jam...?"

She feels a prick of paranoia. She shakes her head for this is indeed her opening scene. Maybe the interest she sensed is not in her at all; maybe this man lurks in the depths of the police station like a fat white spider, waiting to prey on the imaginations of those who come to him for help. She scans his shelves. A dictionary (Webster), also a thesaurus, and next to that *The Elements of Style*. Has she given away too much already?

"Too bad," Smeeth is saying. "Because that would be a beauty. I mean, from the police point of view. You could pinpoint the time of death just by the colour of her skin. Here, I'll give you the number of a guy over in forensic in case you change your mind. But hang on a tick! Now I get it. It's the jam-maker who figures everything out, am I right? She's not the victim after all. She's the one with all the expertise that's going to run circles round the cops. Oh, you writers — I don't know why we don't come to *you*."

This is scary, but it's also like dancing in a way. Look how his mind moves with hers, as if he could reach out and pick her thoughts from the air. Yes, her imaginary sleuth does have exactly the wiles and cranky charm of her boss, Jenny (though Jenny will lose a decade, gain a black silk dress slit from hem to thigh). Has he also figured out the identity of the body in the jam? That Kate herself is that lovely floating body, turning blue? And that the villain is Charlie, the reconstructive surgeon who in the search for perfection has gone one step too far — only to be undone by a woman no one even stops to think has brains, who has the sort of accent that makes people speak very loudly in reply, and who does indeed run rings around the police? Kate is almost moved to share all of this with Smeeth, so they can laugh together at his cleverness and hers.

She allows him just the slim edge of the smile her mother kept for putting people in their place. She taps her pen on her notebook. "What I need to know, precisely, is the procedure once the body is found. Who comes to the scene? How does it go?"

Smeeth slides up an eyebrow. "What time?"

"Nine in the morning."

"Oh excellent. You'll have a new shift, all alert and bushy-tailed. Someone calls 911 of course; then a couple of beat constables hoof it over and confirm. Why not make one of them Chinese as well?"

"As well as what?"

He shrugs. "I'd play up the Chinatown angle, that's all.

Push the local colour — don't forget you're going to want to flog the movie rights."

The movie rights! As if this were the obvious next move, not her most impossible wild dream.

"So tell me," she says, brushing the movie rights aside, "if a second murder was reported the same day, it might seem likely there's a connection?"

"If you put it in, there's bound to be." He gives this the happy look a snake might give a rabbit. "Where's *this* body discovered, by the way?"

"The...bandshell at English Bay?"

"Ah, that will be a radio car that gets that. I'd put a woman in the car, play up the feminine angle. She calls in to the chief of homicide and he says, 'Oh shit, another one...!'"

Oh shit, another one.... She starts scribbling frantically, trying to get down every blessed thing he says. It comes to her that he is treating her as a true professional, that maybe he believes she's who she says. A lovely furry feeling overcomes her as she records how the scene at the jam factory will be secured, the photos taken, the body whisked away. It reminds her of all those times she stood and slowly turned while her mother put pins in the hem of a dress for her. A man who listens or a man who talks, just fine either way. No wonder she fell in love with Fred, who listened to every lying word she had to say. For a second, as she scribbles, she sees how it is all about trust, how the key to everything must be to crack open even if it hurts. Why, if she'd been brave enough she could have linked up with an imaginary chapter of the Guardia Civil, and got herself a secret badge and bright metallic uniform. Perhaps that crazy man was a sign. She could have smiled at him, at least. She does not always have to be above the world. As she takes down what Smeeth details, she is also trying to isolate the smells in this room. The artificial-fibre carpet is the strongest. Smeeth gives off no smell at all. The carpet must be new; it gives off a smell like chloroform. Imagine having your nose squashed into that, the harsh grey twists against your cheek and brow and chin. *Zipped up in plastic bodybag...*, she is writing, *...removed to the morgue.*

"And then the body gets placed in the columbarium,"

Smeeth says. "Now there's a word for you." He waits till she looks up. "That's the room with all the sliding cooler trays."

Something has changed. She feels some rearrangement of the molecules between them. He is expecting her to ask something. Columbarium. All the murdered people, labelled, sealed in plastic, padlocked into steel compartments. If she asked, would he take her there? Does he want to take her there? Smeeth waits, expressionless, head cocked to the side. She is aware of that split between his teeth. She is aware of the small glistening point of his tongue. She feels buoyant, giddy, wary, her bones stuffed with something that is either excitement or disdain, making her springy as a deer. But he will have to ask her decently. (Kate's mother puts the final stitches in a hem, and Kate's date waits below, and Kate takes a twirl.)

The detective glances at his watch. "Well, so then you'll proceed to the autopsy," he says.

She has lost him. She remembers the signs of this, how one minute everything you say is right and the next they can hardly wait to get you off their hands. It is a miracle that Charlie whisked her off to Spanish Banks the night she got chosen Homecoming Queen, and removed the crown and all the rest and she didn't have to say a word.

"And then of course you'll have an inquest," Smeeth is saying. "For example — here's a case that's still unsolved." He swivels back, brings down a file from the shelf behind him. "This is the complete story of an investigation, right here."

A hardboard binder with rings the size of jar lids, the pages surprisingly tattered and brown. The whole thing looks so well-thumbed that Kate feels a warning shiver, not without excitement. *Wait! He pretends to pick a file at random, but this is the one he uses every time.* She finds herself leaning forward with an odd sense of complicity.

"Nice drama," Smeeth says. "Listen." He starts reading out dialogue from an actual inquest. He reads the testimony of the beat constable: how the deceased, Mrs. Juanita Alvarez, was found lying in an alley. He reads the testimony of the doctor: how the knife entered through the chest and again through the stomach, thrusts so powerful they emerged through the lower back. Now he unclips the rings and removes half a dozen glossy photographs. He lays these out across the desk where Kate can see. He sits back, and finally lights his cigarette.

Juanita Alvarez is young. Her skin is very white, her nipples black. Her death is so stark in these black-and-white shots; her body is so lovely otherwise. Just below the breasts, and then again across the soft flesh above her pubic hair, two puckered gashes have been sewn with coarse black thread.

This one's still unsolved. Kate hears the way Smeeth says that, again and again, each time the girl is exposed.

How many times has she been laid out here? Smeeth exhales a rush of nicotine that shoots across the desk, bringing his breath with it. How many times, at this juncture, has he sat back to light his cigarette? Is this a well-known syndrome, the voltage that burns through Kate's body as she looks at the pictures of the girl? She is imagining Smeeth's squat hands, his stubby fingers, his awful whiteness — like those plants you can drink from in the desert if you're dying, the pale rubber of their skin, the bitter release of sickly fluid. If he got up and came around the desk now, she would do any fucking thing he wanted — and what kind of person can she be if that is what such pictures do to her?

⊙▬◄▬ ⊙▬◄▬

She stops walking, finally. She has no idea what to think.

She was only a beat too late, back there. "Oh...!" she said, into that congealed atmosphere. "Oh yes. I see — the knife goes through the ribcage, does it? That must require quite a thrust. The killer would have to be a man, wouldn't you say?"

She asked all the proper questions. If she ever looks into her notebook again, it will all be there.

Smeeth walked her to the elevator, too — and at the last minute jumped in and rode right down with her. "Here, let me give you this," he said. "Maybe you'll be sitting in the middle of the night, and you'll need something right away. Who knows?" He wrote his home phone number on the cover of her notebook crammed with details about bullet trajectories and strangulation marks and the length of time a body takes to cool.

Now she stands absolutely still in the middle of the late-afternoon crowd on Main Street, unaware of people jostling her. *You build things up, and they fall down. That is life's entire plot.*

Someone is looking at her. Someone sees the way shame wells through her body with a force that is going to melt her bones. A man is shuffling towards her, leaning on a cane, a disintegrating man, his skin watery, bloated — though he could be young, he could be Charlie's age. Why is he looking at her as if he knows her? So familiar, that expression — as if he had trailed her all this year, as if he had oozed after her across the wasteland of withdrawal, as if he were another of those apparitions that conjured themselves up out of the aching lack of drink as she lay trembling, wide awake, in the hospital last year.

But this is a person. This is a fellow human being, and now he is peering at her through glasses so thick they are almost yellow, as if he has something important to say.

What does she do to attract these people? Could every bizarre encounter of today have been some sort of trick inside her head, even the seamy aspects of her interview with Smeeth? A product of her needy warped imagination, which can never accept things as they are but must always make them worse?

Maybe Smeeth was a perfectly nice man, trying to do his job. Maybe he was as lonely as she was.

What if she did call him, late one night? Late one night, in the morgue-like silence of her room, what if she got him on the line?

Now this damaged man has stopped right in front of her.

Of course. He wants money. He is not here to reveal some further dismal fact about herself. Money is what he wants.

All she has is a twenty-dollar bill, and bus fare — all she has in the world until she gets the current batch of aprons done. Well then! She will give him everything she has. This thought has trouble squeezing out, but it leaves her limp and saved. The gift will be for herself, of course, in the manner of most offerings.

"Excuse me," he says, "could you help me across that corner down there?" He points back in the direction of the police station. "I have to get to the bus stop."

So he is here to point out a further lack in her, after all. For look how she recoils. Why her? *Why me?* Why not those businessmen in pinstripes who have just sidled out of Number Five, one with his fly undone?

She thinks what her mother would have done. Without one moment's hesitation, even dead and gone, her mother would pass by on the other side.

She tucks her bracelet up inside her sleeve, holds out her arm.

The man reaches barely to her ear, but before she has a chance to resist he forces his arm through hers and grabs her hand. This is a strength she knows from dreams. His hand settles into hers, palm to palm, such an intimate connection. His thick eyes goggle up at her.

"Do you have trouble seeing?" she asks. "Is that why you need help?"

"No," he says simply. "I have trouble walking. I'm afraid I'll fall down."

A bus pulls away from that far stop. "I hope that wasn't *your* bus," she says.

"It doesn't matter. Any bus will do. I only came down here for the meeting. I'm trying to break a really bad addiction. Fifteen years. Every time I get clear, I go under again."

Oh lord, and the man reeks of years of desolation, a smell so hollow and awful it has the strength of an undertow — and floating on top of that, the sweet dank odour of an afternoon spent drinking beer.

This is crazy. His breath is misting up her cheek. His hand rests in hers, like a small hot animal. *Every time I get clear, I go under again.* She has walked with her children this way. They will never remember that, now. She would have given her lifeblood for them. Did that prevent her from doing things so weak and ugly it will take them their whole lives to get over her?

She stops and jerks her arm free. He will never get clear. What is the point of getting clear? Even sober and straight he will still be a half-blind cripple, afraid of falling down. She gives him a fast fake smile as he stands wobbling there. "I'm sorry. I realized I'm late for an appointment." He is staring meekly, as if he knew from the start that this was what she'd do. Then she catches something further in his expression, something sly.

Her hand is sticky where he held it. She walks away very fast. Some dreadful sticky substance has transferred itself from his hand to hers, and she can feel those raw places on her fingers, all that shredded skin, those little half-healed wounds. Oh Jesus, she says, oh ugh, oh Christ. She will have to go straight over to Jenny's and scrub her hands with bleach.

She almost runs across the street, against the yellow light. But when she gets to the other side she has to turn and look back. He is where she left him, staring after her. He raises that hand.

⊙═◄ ⊙═◄

Shadows take on a different character at a certain time of afternoon. I deal in shadows, but even I find that so. I have just spent six months of my life capturing shadows with my camera, then marshalling them into patterns, turning those patterns into stencils, printing the stencils onto silk. It seemed a good thing, at that time of my life (I began the project when I had recently left what I thought was love behind), to be able to tame shadows. The order I sent off to New York this afternoon contained the whole of those months' work, fifteen bolts printed with the webbed and tangling silhouettes of huckleberry, mountain ash, alder leaves, ferns. Now the shadow of my piano is a flattened tongue advancing slowly across my bare hardwood floor.

I can imagine how shadows looked to Kate that afternoon on Main Street, shadows flopping over curbs, peeling onto the road, becoming slick dark conduits that might carry you along. Don't all of us suspect there's a place we could broach if we only had the nerve and the light was right? You walk an echoing corridor that spirals down. You enter a locked room. Wonder of wonders, everything is labelled; you just need to find the right drawer, slit the plastic, and at last you're face to face with who you are. Then, instead, imagine staring in and in and finding merely a lack so great that all the sweetness of the world is not enough. Nothing will fill this, though of course you have to try.

When Charlie pushed her down the stairs, it seemed that Kate had been awaiting just such a final thing for years. Look at him, cracking free of his shell of irreproachable behaviour. Every unhappiness she had known or imagined was finally justified in that moment when Charlie grabbed her by the shoulders shouting, *Why are you doing this, why, why, WHY?* That was the shame of it, that was what scared her — that she could exert such power and bring it crashing back upon herself, and for one moment feel truly alive. That was what she could never tell the therapist.

And Charlie wanted her back, that was another thing she never told. He wanted her back no matter what. She would be able to do anything, drink oceans, have delusions, goodness knows. She was his wife. He was a responsible man of medicine. From now on though, forever, he would never again pay Kate the attention he had paid her the day he pushed her down the stairs.

Against all of that, she has spent her whole year of freedom struggling. She has stored up not just boxes of details about crime, but words, treasure chests of words that any day she will melt into shining sentences. Sometimes, when she is doing other things, those words arrange themselves. Sometimes she drops what she is doing, takes out her typewriter, puts a fresh piece of paper in, keeping her eye on the lovely artifact that has just appeared before her eyes, that product of *her* mind, hers, a sudden glimmer through the silt of her everyday concerns. But every time she plunges in to take it, she comes up with a dented hubcap, or an old rubber boot.

Disgusting, awful, awful, Kate says, as she hurries along Main Street, away from the crippled man. What a mess in the end, this day — harassed by madmen and lewd policemen, and shamed into giving her arm to perverts with god knows what on their hands. Such a dupe she was — so unable to refuse, so superstitious. So afraid of falling down. But she is reaching out for all that now, she is gathering it in. Awful, awful. Look how she's tried and tried, and look where she is. The air around her glitters with triumphant awfulness, as final as when her husband last put his hands on her. No one should have to suffer this.

At Jenny's she will ask for money. This is not the impulse of a moment — no, she understands, all at once, that it has been in her head all day long, a clever plan of escape should the day go wrong. And look at her, a jittering wreck, useless to the world; twenty dollars is never going to get her where she needs to go.

At Jenny's she will plead dire emergency, maybe a family illness in a foreign city like Toronto, requiring a round-trip ticket, a considerable sum. She starts calculating odds. If she asks Jenny for five hundred, will she end up with three? Well, she thinks, I can even pawn my bracelet, come to that.

She has started shaking but that hardly matters, it's just a stage along the way. Her veins flood with the splendid golden weakness of this moment when she's arrived, without thought or conscious choice, on the other side of all the barriers.

And as for me, I killed my child so I could keep my lover. That is the short story of my life.

He did not make me do it. "Look, it's your decision" was all he said, "but you can't" — his anguished persecuted look — "surely you do not expect me to stay around and help you raise it, that's all. You have always known how I felt."

Yes, I had certainly known that he had a horror of other people's children. It wasn't just the noise and fuss, it was a more basic fear than that. He felt the very essence of himself assaulted by the small shrill voices and the clutter of baby packs and strollers and fuzzy toys and soothers which, one by one, the few couples we were friends with had succumbed to. "We have a perfect life, Mariel," he'd often said as he fled some gathering of colleagues and their partners, the fathers with snugglies on their chests, *like goddamn emasculated kangaroos,* as he put it. "How thankful I am for the calm and sanity of the life I lead with you."

He was my husband of seven years, this man I still speak of as my lover. He was a solitary man, and when we met I felt such a jolt of recognition — as if I'd had the extraordinary luck of coming upon a missing part of myself — that I became his double as nearly as I could. I allowed him to build a cage for me out of air, and for seven years I sheltered there. I thought that if he ever left me I would die.

Of course I did not try to conceive a child. After a time I began to believe, in any case, that no baby would be kind enough to come and rest in that dry sack of mine. I was completely unprepared for the shock of life settling inside me. It was only then I understood that I had forgotten there was such a thing as joy.

No, he did not make me do it. But after I had done it, I could not stand to look at his essential face again.

That is an old story now. I try not to dwell on it. I work. Usually I thank whatever fates there are that I have the need to do this, and that I am good at what I do. I work, and live alone. I was never pretty. I recognize that there is no escape for me. Still, I can't give up the hope that out of the patience and skill and care my narrow life requires, will come the thing that saves me — grace, I suppose I mean.

Sometimes though, on days like this, I wish I had the courage to abandon hope completely — to imagine, if even for a moment, that I might just let go and blaze and burn, and it wouldn't matter after that, nothing would matter; I would rise from the ashes, or not. It would be completely out of my hands.

And so I watch Kate Rutherford, at the close of that chill March afternoon. She has taken a taxi from the jam factory back to the west side of the city. I see her stand for a moment

on the curb, trying to give the impression of a woman un-
hurried, normal, calm. I watch as she follows the driver up
the stairs to her tiny dim apartment. He sets a carton by the
phone. Will she ask him to stay? It will never cross her mind.
She will be trembling, but she will take the time to look into
the mirror, where she will see herself as merry and beautiful
and bad.

The door will close. The first bottle will be opened. And
words will flow through her like a serum, and the room will
fill with evening with no one to turn on the light — only
Kate, floating like a lily, borne upon the surface of that delicious murmuring.

DO YOU REALLY LOVE ME?

"Do you love me?" she says.

"Yes," he says.

"But really?" she says. "Shawn, really? Are you sure?"

The woman conducting the interrogation is Margareta. She is standing in the kitchen of her West Vancouver home, in front of a dark green Aga cooker, holding a free-range egg.

"Yes I love you," he says. "I love you absolutely." He is a scientist. He uses words with some precision. *I love you absolutely.* What is that supposed to mean?

He is sitting at the table, poised on the brink of restlessness. He is like a nice hunting dog, she used to say — that deep red hair, though somewhat prematurely grizzled, and that quick response to signals not everyone can hear, and a maddening way of sliding his gaze off to the horizon when she needs to hold his eye. She hears his stomach grumble now, underneath his jeans, his zebra-printed jockey shorts. She sees his nose twitch.

She brings the eggs to the table, her movements consciously slow. She knows she is an exceptional-looking woman. She is tall, with features that clearly show her Viking ancestry, the excellent bones, the long pale hair. Her shape carves an empty space out of the air.

The sun slants through the french windows, and strikes the cut-glass marmalade jar. Light spills across the pale oak table in a webbed and shifting pool, and the shadow of the marmalade jar falls across this, cut exactly as the glass is cut, yet black as black, shot with stars.

He has been making love to her. His tongue has just traced the inside of her thigh. She lies with every inch of her front fused to every inch of the back of him, so she can feel his heartbeat, his breathing, each twitch and ripple of his skin.

"But do you find me interesting?" she says. "Do I still fill your mind the way you told me once I did? Like an expanding flower."

"Oh shit," he says. "Yes, you interest me. Now for Christ's sake, Margareta, let's get some sleep."

The brain of the man whose tongue has just traced the inside of her thigh would be declared a national treasure in some countries, wrapped in velvet, accorded every sort of care and cosseting. But still his thoughts would go free.

Margareta is a weaver, not a scientist. She dyes silks and weaves them into ikat-patterned yardages that get sewn into clothing for the very very rich. She is a colourist by instinct. Still, she is not disorganized. She conducts experiments, makes samples, keeps records, knows how to fracture the rainbow and put the whole thing back again. But she is not a scientist. She engages in a craft that teeters on the rim of magic. She finds what she does extremely interesting, and she would like to tell her husband things. But when she explains how pumpkin rinds, if boiled and boiled, will render the exact colour of the pelt of a vicuña, how if you boil them one extra minute you get silt, "Yes," he says. Sometimes he looks so lonely when he says this. She wishes she understood his work.

"It's not that you wouldn't understand," he lies. "If I explained you would understand as well as I do. But Margareta, I'm thinking of these things all day. When I come home, I like to talk of something else."

This is a relief, though it drives her wild. It makes her head ache and she feels suffocated, thinking of the effort that would be required to track the spirals of his reasoning, in and in. But she would like to creep along the hallways of his head, all the same. She pictures rows and rows of backlit cases lined with velvet, sealed with glass. She would like to see what fills the shadows in between.

His work is all to do with chaos. Perhaps that is why he has become so taciturn. He works with fractals, those curves that lie at the heart, somehow, of an understanding of the chaos of the universe. He has a new assistant called Vera Willson-Baum.

He has a new assistant who is young, blonde in the way that baby ducks are, with downy skin and feathered hair — eyes like torn scraps of sky, revealing how she has been hurt once and will take, in consequence, anything she needs. A scientist, of course. It is the job of this young, blonde, hyphenated assistant to put Margareta's husband's delicate understanding of the chaos of the universe into computer words.

Margareta lies in the dark and listens to the wind rush through the cedars, the waves crash on the rocks, the mournful regular exhaling of the foghorn from Point Atkinson; she listens to the fathoms of her husband's breathing, and when at last she slides beneath the waves she dreams she has found a way to peel the rind from his skull.

Margareta has been eating poison. This is the sickly sweetness her dreams have left on her. She walks the shore. She examines what the sea brings in, the plastic, the few green living strands.

What does it matter if he loves her or he doesn't? Why should all the fibres in her head be tied to just one man, an assemblage of atoms, nothing more? The sun is shining, and when he is gone and she is gone and even when the ozone layer is gone the sun will still be there. And when all of them are gone, the earth will heal.

Do you love me? she says. *Yes*, he says. Sometimes he smiles. Sometimes he takes her in his arms, takes her to their bed, fills all her empty spaces with flesh. But she will never crack the circle of bone that shields his brain, as in her dreams.

She could rise above this, fly.

She hunkers down against a log. The sea glitters with a crust of silver, like something Liberace might have worn.

Her work is changing. In the dye-bath the rough silk strands are becoming glossier and at the same time absorbing brackish halftones, yet she is not doing one thing different than she has always done.

There has been a downturn in the economy, but her sales have not dropped off. Rather, women flock from West End penthouses to the show room where her fabrics are displayed. Beautiful women, who buy and buy. High-class tarts and drugs are making her rich. Good, she says.

Vera Willson-Baum decides that she would like to get to know Margareta, get to know her better that is, go out to lunch and things. Vera Willson-Baum is looking for a *pal?*

"Well, you know, she doesn't have it easy," says Shawn. "She is raising that kid all by herself, and then the long hours she puts in at work — why shouldn't she want a pal?" Margareta catches his look before it darts off to the side.

Margareta and Shawn are supposed to be doing a late-winter garden cleanup. But Shawn is about to carve their laurel hedge into a row of topiary animals. They have no real garden at all, just a hillside of rocks and ferns and arbutus and huckleberry and salal, natural, entirely suitable, with that hedge that screens them from the road. Suddenly Shawn has taken it into his head to make of this a row of rabbits, ducks and hens. There is no telling him this won't work. He intends to reduce the entrance of their private domain to order and to cuteness. He works with chaos. He intends to reduce the entrance of their home to shapes that might amuse a child.

Shawn bends as if to fire up the chainsaw, but instead straightens and turns back — the same man she's always known: plaid shirt from the Army and Navy, old frayed jeans, duck boots. Probably he has been fooling her with this business of topiary. They will laugh. He will saw up a fallen tree.

"The thing is, Vera admires you," he says pleasantly. "She is so impressed by the way you have structured your life with-

out children or distractions — the way you let nothing inter-
fere with the hours when you work, even though you work
alone."

His eyes are speckled, lovely as the backs of speckled trout,
as they flick to meet hers, flick away. If she came up close she
would smell the familiar smell, a little dark and boggy no
matter how much clean water and aftershave. If she came up
close she would want to lie down, right there, in the bushes.
He is a collection of faults, and she has been hooked by them.

"Vera loves your fabric, too," Shawn is saying. "She says
it is exactly what she would wear — well, of course, if she
could afford that sort of thing."

If she could afford that sort of thing. Every penny she earns
goes on the child, naturally.

Margareta is standing with one foot in a muddy puddle,
and her boot has sprung a leak and her sock is wicking up the
chill, but if she notices it is only to observe what she can
endure. Let the record show, she wants to shout, that it was a
mutual decision not to have children. We didn't fudge, either. We didn't say, "You're not doing a kid a favour to bring
it into this world." We lived for art and science and each other,
all according to plan.

Yet now Shawn's heart is being tugged by the damp diaper-
filled air of Willson-Baum's apartment, is that it? Time is folded
there so bravely, and still that woman manages to link arms
with another woman's husband and escort him along his in-
tellectual path. And Margareta cannot say a thing. For maybe
she has it wrong. Maybe when he says he is working late he is
really working. Maybe everything is the way it always was,
and it is only that she has caught a splinter, as in "The Snow
Queen." In the eye or in the heart.

So they arrange to go out to dinner, Margareta and
Willson-Baum. Margareta is going to slice open her heart and
cast out doubt, suspicion, fear. She is no fool; her work is
becoming more and more hideous and beautiful, and her gut
is becoming permanently twisted, and on her face, just below the surface, a network of lines is waiting to break out.

She considers her outfit for the evening very carefully.
She selects at last a shirt and narrow pants of dove-grey leather,

sleek lizard Bruno Magli shoes, a long red coat lined with fur. She is not sure why she has chosen to cover herself in the teguments of other creatures. She rims her eyes with smoky shadow. Her eyes are the green of Roman glass, the green of the sea. She runs an antique comb of tortoiseshell through her hair. Her hair fans in a full crimped tangle, only just controlled. She coats her lips in gloss the colour of the pale centre of a strawberry, accents the hollows beneath her excellent cheekbones with a stick of bronze and then — a trick she has learned — runs a swath of this same colour across her forehead, down the bridge of her nose, like war-paint. When this is blended she looks fierce and beautiful and sun-loved, and none of it matters a damn.

Vera Willson-Baum wears a dress about as stylish as a lab coat, shoes from Zellers, a macramé hat that has been passed down to her by an aunt who was a hippie. The outside of her is so very young and soft that even Margareta would like to touch her. Margareta's fingers, for a moment, have grown her husband's skin. She imagines the soft whirring noise the girl's brain would make, the girl's body trembling.

The idea was that they would have a drink and then decide where to go for dinner — somewhere casual, alighting like swallows on the whim of the moment, that was the plan. But Vera Willson-Baum turns out to be very heavy going. She knows exactly where she stands in the scheme of everything. She knows all about Shawn's work, which of course is her work too. She knows it is the only thing worth knowing. She talks so lucidly about the work that it would be possible to learn many useful things, except that Margareta is listening through a scrim of jealousy. Margareta nods and smiles a lot. Her face hurts.

She steers her guest to an Indonesian restaurant where they can sit at a U-shaped counter and watch the chef, a short dark man in a tall white hat, a magician it seems. He takes chickens, vegetables, fish, and transforms them into tiny chunks which he stir-fries, sauces, flames. Every few minutes the room goes dark, and he performs a strobe-lit juggling act with his long sharp knives.

Why does Margareta do it? She could have made it through

the entire evening as safely as a charming (paying) clam. Instead she asks about Vera Willson-Baum's baby. Something about the juggling brought this on. "How do you manage?" she asks. "It must be so demanding, working the long hours that you do, *and* raising a son."

"Yes," Vera Willson-Baum says. Her eyelashes are finer than spider webs. "But my boy is five years old now. He is starting kindergarten."

So there won't be diapers. There will be playdough animals, and big childish drawings on the fridge, and Shawn will be struck by the exuberant creativity of children while this woman who is a child herself gets out the cups and saucers for the peppermint tea.

"Still, of course it is difficult," Vera Willson-Baum says. Such a look of sadness waxes, wanes, as in the strobe-lights her profile comes and goes. "But I was so young when I decided to keep him. I was barely twenty. And I thought" — she snaps her fingers — "I thought I could manage it just like that. I thought I knew everything."

And it is not so much that Margareta is moved to compassion. No, she is dashing up the spiral of a lonely tower of her own, dashing towards the parapet — and the soles of her feet tingle, and her stomach flutters with the anticipation of leaping into space, naked, it doesn't matter, reaching out for once and touching the mind of someone else. "God yes," she hears herself admit, "it really is an amazing process, growing older." Just saying "growing older" sets her teeth on edge, but it is thrilling all the same, this giving herself away. "It's like having a chair pulled out from under you. Such a surprise!" She smiles at Vera Willson-Baum, really smiles, it doesn't even hurt. She bends forward, bursting now. "For example, I know the work I do is good — but for a long time I've been wanting to do something more. I should be a painter, you know. I've got the potential for something really great inside." She carries on, revealing herself ridiculously, saying far too much, though Vera Willson-Baum is staring past her ear. "I want to say things with my art that could move the world the way the music of Mozart, painted out on canvas, could. But just last night, in the middle of the night, I was struck by a paralysing thought. In less than ten years I will be fifty. And who *cares* what a fifty-year-old woman has to say?"

Vera Willson-Baum turns and blinks. "My," she says, "I wonder where that was coming from." Her eyes are blank and Margareta sees herself reflected, reduced to bite-sized twins. In the background the chef is dismembering a chicken. He turns his knife upon an onion and the globe falls apart into a flower.

Margareta stands on the path above the yacht harbour and listens to sounds braided by the wind. She has been walking and walking a circle route that takes her along this path, then down along the shore and past her house, and then loops back here again. Hours and hours. All at once she understands how infinity is curved. She, emaciated, wild-haired Margareta, who is either being betrayed by her husband or making it all up, is as close to the logic of the chaos of the universe as anyone. Shawn will not get any closer. Vera Willson-Baum will not get any closer. She, soaked-to-the-skin Margareta, is both the centre and the rim.

She is gorgeous for a moment, ripped open by the beauty of the vision, which even as she stares just fades. Rain slides across her eyes. She is left standing, such a speck, such a fool.

My, I wonder where that was coming from.

Margareta has set her looms on fire. She took them apart piece by piece, all the hand-turned parts of wood that a carpenter on Denman Island fashioned to her exact specifications some fifteen years ago — out of oak, a wood not easy to destroy, as Margareta discovered when she began cutting them up into fireplace-sized pieces yesterday. She started with the handsaw, but soon went to fetch the smaller of the two power saws she and Shawn had used when they were building the house. Thanks to technology, then, cutting up the looms and various accoutrements — the spinners, the inkle looms for belts, the Salish loom made from branches she herself cut from a silver birch tree — took not much more than half an hour. The wood was neatly stacked beside the acorn stove in her studio, and when Shawn came in to kiss her — late, as has been his pattern these days — he rubbed his hands together and said, "Hey, you've got yourself some nice-looking wood, way to go." They went out to the kitchen. He helped her improvise a pasta. He had promised to bring home fresh snapper and some prawns, but of course he had forgotten.

Today it is raining once again. The loom makes an ample blaze, and Margareta is seated cross-legged on the rug. She is cutting up all her weavings now. What a silken nest of colour she is making, as she slashes with her long black-handled shears.

She is a woman deformed, though it still does not show. She has felt the actual physical effects, her face squeezed triangular, her whole torso made wide and flat and hard, to accommodate a ladder of iron bars. It is remarkable that she is able to bend into her cross-legged position by the fire. But when she turns to her new work, things ease.

She has found a higher discipline at last, by merest accident. She was cutting some yardage from the loom yesterday morning, when a sudden flash of Shawn's face — smiling, as he so often is, for no clear reason — caused the scissors to jump off at a diagonal and slash across the cloth. She watched as the strands began to unravel, the threads breaking free and flaring like the petals of slim flowers. *Deconstruction.* That slithered through her head, such a silly word, yet she let it take the air and saw how it gave a stamp of recognition. I am a deconstructionist, she said.

So now she sits amid a heap of threaded colour. And she is a wizard of colour. There is no secret of the spectrum hidden from her. She knows that if you collapse the rainbow you get black, not blinding white as is supposed.

She is not sure what happens after this, how much farther she must go.

How Margareta smiled to think that she, unaided, had got chaos theory in a nutshell, art and science marvellously twinned — reverse alchemy. By its practice anything might be made acceptable, even the whole fleeing sky.

Instead, she is helping Shawn make watermelon pickle, on a sunny Saturday.

They make this pickle every year, when the first new melons come in from Mexico. He won a prize once for his watermelon pickle. Naturally she had assumed this year would be different, but yesterday he came home early, bringing a basketful of melons from Chinatown and two new wooden-handled cleavers, his and hers.

"Listen," he said, "I'm sick of that damn lab. I've been overdoing it, I guess. In any case, it's the weekend and I don't intend even to answer the phone."

At first she felt weak, hit by a wave of relief and gratitude. It had all been nothing. Or if there had been something, it was over. He was here. She was safe.

Last night he was consistently attentive. So now we have this fine domestic scene.

The relief has ebbed, and she tries this on — there is nothing to fear. Can she survive without those gulps of fear?

He sterilizes jars, she scrubs the table for chopping, he whistles while he works. "I've been thinking," he says suddenly. "We lead rather self-centred lives. Well, I do. Maybe we should make some changes."

Anything could be hiding in the shadows of the next few moments. But why shouldn't it be good? Maybe we make our own fate, by never allowing the next thing to be good. Maybe, if she concentrates all her mind and heart upon it, he will turn and see her — truly see, truly her — and she will feel his perception burning awfulness away, and she will look back along that beam, and everything about him will be revealed.

"Maybe we should get a puppy," he says.

"Well," he says, into the silence where the puppy dropped, "from now on I intend to work at home more. I could help train it." He is busy lifting out the steaming jars with tongs, arranging them on a green-striped cloth. He has a smile on his face, like an appealing little boy.

"What are you thinking?" she asks, keeping her voice soft, very soft.

His gaze slides out to sea, though there is nothing out

there but a shifting net of mirrors.

"What are you thinking?" she asks, once again. "What are you smiling at?"

"Oh, just the peaceful easy feeling," he says, humming it. That old Eagles refrain — one of their favourites, long ago. "I'm thinking this is perfect," he says. "I'm thinking how when I'm with you, the world disappears." He comes around and tries to nuzzle the nape of her neck. "My beautiful sphinx." He ruffles her hair absently. "I will never understand you, but I don't even feel I have to try."

Margareta takes hold of a melon and lets fly with her cleaver. The halves split apart, revealing shimmering flesh, shining seeds. You can tell a lot about a melon once you have split it. You can count the seeds and compute the future generations. You can taste the flesh and understand about the soil, the weather, everything.

He is looking at her. He has backed up to the sink and he is looking at her, and for a moment she thinks it is all going to be all right, after all.

EVOLUTION

Elephants are clouds that have been sentenced to earth.

Terry Gambril, who does not sleep well any more, caught that this morning before the six o'clock news, on a program rebroadcast from Australia, where they have more to say than you might believe on any number of strange things. He turned the kitchen radio low so as not to wake his wife. After a twitch of hesitation he fished out the pack of cigarettes hidden in his toolbox by the door. Anyway, if Penelope got up now and came through, "Silly old thing" would be all she'd say. *Silly old thing, you know the doctor told you not to do that.* When they lived down in their old house, they used to have a dog who took to chewing up the oriental rugs, and she would tell off that good old dog in the same absent-minded tone.

But maybe she would come up close instead, imperious and vague — maybe she would take the cigarette right from his lips, so close that he could smell her hair, a smell that was not shampoo but something acrid and compelling, like walnut leaves, he was thinking now, the pungent smell when you hunted through them on your knees. And maybe he would grab her wrist.

Most mornings as he is waking he thinks that none of this has happened: Platt hasn't pulled the old house down; Terry isn't thrashing in a single cot in what he used to call the hired man's house — a washed-up geezer of not even fifty, with a wife lying like a curled-up statue in her own narrow cot across the room. Before he starts trying to crawl back down the tunnel of sleep, he has a moment when he sees the gabled ceiling of the old place, and for a cruel half-second, stained-glass windows seem to float in front of dingy fibreboard, and he is looking through a puzzle of clear and coloured light to where the hills are pulling themselves out of shadow, across the lake.

Is that how it is for Penelope, as well? *Is that why you sleep with your head underneath the pillow, and not because of how I snore?* When that thought butted into him this morning, he stopped in the middle of the kitchen and steeled himself for more. A familiar glassy emptiness fell over him instead. Then from behind the curtain he heard Penelope's bedsprings give a squeak. Quickly he ducked into the cupboard where she kept her few remaining valued things, and helped himself to a sketchbook with marbled covers, a ribbon to tie it closed, *which I gave to you in the first place, so why not? You never even untied the ribbon; just kept pouring all that fine work out on newsprint — gone for good now, for all you cared!* He grabbed the pen from by the phone, a wrecked ballpoint advertising Okanagan Feed and Chemical. *Anyway by the time you're up and wrinkling your lovely nose, I'll be long gone out to the shack on the hill, summing up my fortunes.*

Grand phrase.

But I must have saved at least a bale of those drawings, he was thinking. He had a sudden urge to go out and root through the trunks in the toolshed where all that stuff had ended up, as if her drawings might be the only clue he'd ever get to what was going on inside of her. *Silly old thing.* She never blamed him, not out loud. "You take her or any of her sisters," he was muttering as he unsnapped the shirt he'd done up wrong and started over, "every one of those girls hitched up with some bright-eyed guy who thought he'd help himself to a slice of family pie and à-la-mode it, and yet they still drift along in their own little pride-filled clouds." He could put it that way if he wanted, if it helped. How would she react if he went in now and shook her awake and confessed the outrageous half-assed idea that had struck him yesterday — worthy of the old Terry for sure, that wild kid who, the first time he ever got up the courage to ask Penelope Murdoch out, decided to twiddle a wire or two on some helpful stranger's car so he could take the drive out along the lake.

Yesterday he had been down on Platt's wharf, working away at his long-term project of tweezering it apart, nail by nail. That wharf is an affront to nature and human decency, and if you take it together with the house that Platt also built on the beach, after knocking down the Murdoch place, it is obvious that every time Lilian Platt sends him down to firm up the struts, Terry should pop out a couple of nails for every one he hammers in — which was what he was up to yesterday when a blinding zigzag struck, a flash that actually lit up Platt's powerboat where it was moored just below.

So I've figured a way out of all my problems, Pen. What a laugh. She would shake her head, half smiling, wouldn't she? Just like that first time when he cruised out and tried to coax her for a drive, he would never quite know if she had heard.

He poured a jet of milk into his bowl of cornflakes and the drainboard was suddenly awash; and as the crispy little flakes went floating into the sink, a scattering of memories broke loose and followed, down to the depths, where he could feel them start soaking in his guilt and blackness, all the stuff he had to keep a lid on: swelling, growing plump with pain.

November, a year and a half ago. The beach below the old house adrift in leaves rimmed with frost. Penelope getting a huge bonfire going. She has just found out that Platt is going to demolish that fine old place her grandad built. Look how almost merry she is, tossing on her father's papers, everything: her dark hair slipping from its knot, her eyes flashing that yellow light, her jeans all smudged, almost singed. Now she has pitched on a box of her drawings, but Terry snatches it back. She aims to get rid of his books as well, and the children's stuff he has hung onto for so long — but this is before his stroke, when he retains shreds of his old stubbornness and pride. She is destroying pieces of history that should have gone to the museum, for sure — all those boxes from the attic, stuffed so full that when the twine is cut the contents blossom out, the brownish envelopes and title deeds and letters, even her great-grandad's journal from when he first rode into the Okanagan along the fur brigade trail. Dreamily she watches the charred remnants flutter on the updraft, then mashes them with the pointed stick she holds to control the fire.

Elephants move through the jungles of the world in marvellous silence, despite their mounded, piled-up size. That is why they are compared to clouds. Also, according to old Sri Lankan legend, they used to live in the skies. And like most of us, they fell. And like most of us, they fell for reasons they would never understand. Three of them had been soaring over the jungle on the wings they still had then, admiring the way the trees whipped and snapped when they passed low, but getting bored, finally. And exactly at that moment, they looked down into a clearing and saw the Lord Buddha surrounded by a ring of students, all cross-legged on the ground. Silently those huge grey shapes swooped into a tree. They perched on a branch, in a row, leaning forward eagerly. Of course the branch came crashing down. Seven of the students were killed. As punishment, ever since, elephants have been born without wings.

News, weather, sports, after that — turned so low the excited morning-radio voices bounced around like gnats. Out of long-time habit Terry strained to hear the weather. What did the day hold for the cherry crop? Though what was that to him? Platt's trees now. Platt's crop — Platt's bumper crop, as fate would have it, after the years of rain that had wiped out the likes of Terry. How did it happen that the Platts of this life had fortune so damn tickled while some other man might have the necessary qualities and then some, yet there was one screw missing so the whole thing just seized up, and you never got to discover what that one screw was? Useless to waste energy on thoughts like that — which could have been the root of his problems, how all his life he'd be one place in his head and then the next, a monkey of a guy, certainly the despair of his principal back in school, *You have the marks, Gambril, but the committee has decided to give the bursary to Smith.* Poor Mr. Klassen, his turtle head poking forward, his kind eyes blinking.

And Terry in reply: *That's all right sir, thank you. I'm getting married, anyway.* A monkey of a guy to pull that one off, for sure — just look at the unlikely high school hero cruising out in pursuit, his hands numb in the unheated jalopy he has liberated from in front of the beer parlour on Main Street. And then the warmth of the big old house. Even from the hallway, the view of the lake broken into chunks of reflected firelight, and him not letting himself feel awed as Penelope leads him through into a room with high beamed ceilings, panelled walls, a flattened grizzly by the fire; a room full of girls, all with the same high-bridged noses, like a flock of snooty little hawks — and here is Terry lounging with one elbow on the mantel, till his basketball jacket starts giving off a frizzled smell. *This is how it's done. This is how my old man used to do it, back in the old country, before his family gave him the heave-ho.* The wry little purse of her mouth, when he finally gets up the courage to ask her for a drive. The yellowy amber of her eyes. The way her eyes turn down at the corners when she smiles, the laughter sealed inside. Then the smell of her coat, still trailing the camphorated breath of the mullion-windowed closet in the hall — and the way, in the sudden rush of February air, her nose is turning red at the end, so that he almost reaches out to touch it, to see if this means hot or cold. "I thought we'd go for a hike." Penelope is evading altogether the issue of the stolen car. "I'll take you up to see our famous hundred-dollar view."

Terry brought himself back reluctantly to a struggle with his khaki work pants, which had been hanging above his boots on the peg by the kitchen door. They fell to the ground more than once before he got them belted, and he saw that he'd scattered little worms of ash on the floor. *And after she's swept that up, she'll be looking out her rubber gloves and heading down to Platt's, won't she? No stopping her.* Keeping up the damn essential deal she'd pulled while Terry was still helpless in the hospital, which allowed them to go on living on the place. And if he ever complained that Platt ought to get someone else in to do the really heavy cleaning, she'd just say, *Hush, look how generous they've been, we could be living in some trailer park in town.*

Through all these thoughts and counter-thoughts, those elephants were flapping, those tragedians, those clowns. Maybe they had just wanted to hear a good story, those big clumsy guys. But maybe they had truly hoped to touch the quivering centre of the wisdom of the world.

⊙⇥⇤ ⊙⇥⇤

Once Penelope's great-grandfather owned all this land above the cliffs, about as far as you can see. That was when you could run cattle from one end of the valley to the other, not a fence, not an orchard or a vineyard, just desert country, bunch grass and sage.

Terry has climbed to the old pickers' shack, directly above the block of cherries he planted fifteen years ago. *Our famous hundred-dollar view.* That was what they called it, those Murdochs, because from exactly this spot the photograph was taken that for years was on the hundred-dollar bill. The lake stretches north in a breathtaking sweep. The clay cliffs dazzle the eyes. Clouds shift and jostle above the bony hills, but today the sky stays hot and blue. Each leaf glistens as it rustles over every other leaf, and the trunks and branches of the cherry trees gleam with that elusive silvered purple that can catch at his heart, no matter how down he is. The pattern that your trees make. He used to think of that as the pattern of his future stretching down the hill, following the humps and hollows, laid out in hopeful generous rows.

A group of pickers is moving into the tree directly below the shack — two men, a woman, a little girl. The child is wearing green cord overalls, a ninja shirt. She is chattering away in what must be Vietnamese.

The Platts moved up here from Vancouver because — as Lilian Platt puts it — she did not care to see her kids carved up or shot. "Not that you can really blame those boys in the Asian gangs," she was explaining, when he was down there helping Penelope with the windows the other day. "I caught this professor on a talk show saying how they're part of a lost generation, so desensitized they're hardly human any more, which explains the drive-by shootings, I guess, and the house invasions! It's a tragedy. But the point is" — jamming her hands on her hips to block Penelope from edging towards the deck to get some air — "why should it be *our* tragedy?" If you pointed out how her crop is being taken off today, she would just bend your ear in a different direction, perhaps about the agricultural-land-freeze bureaucracy. A neighbour, old Joe Boratto, has agreed to run the place until Platt can get the property eased out, and Joe swears by his efficient crews of former refugees.

Terry hasn't been out to the shack since Platt took over. He had to bat yards of cobwebs from the glass before he could pry the casement open to blow away the empty-shack smell. Then he dragged the table over to the window. After that, he got lost for a while. He watched the evolution of the clouds. He thought of those elephants once more. He saw them settling down on a branch, in a row.

Now he follows the blue of the lake right to where it skirts Rattlesnake Point. And all at once his head is pulsing with a wild electric buzz. This is just like yesterday. The whole landscape is jittering with a halo of outrageous possibility, and again he is seeing Platt's powerboat making a break for it up the lake — a bullet through the centre of a calm and peaceful scene. The Sea Ray. Which Terry never even gets to touch of course, though it's okay to let him tinker with the Jet Skis. The world comes to an end if those kids of Platt's can't be churning up the water. That boat, metallic red, with the hand-built racing engine that alone set Platt back some ninety thousand bucks, as he's quick to say. The finest sleekest pointed object that ever slipped into your dreams.

The horror on all the Platt faces as they follow that red streak, as they take in a distant burst of flame.

⊙═‹‹‹ ⊙═‹‹‹

Terry was just nineteen when he married smack into the middle of the hundred-dollar view. Just nineteen, a nervy kid. A bushel of years ago. But even in the hospital last year, in dirty-trick dreams, he would find himself back listening to the rustle not so much of money as of glorious accomplishment to come — what he would do, himself, Terry Gambril, now that he'd landed in the situation where old man Murdoch had to give him a chance, how he would buy more land, and more and more, and make it fruitful, never mind if he overextended just a bit — no longer just the son of poor Jed Gambril, *that charming man,* as they said at the end, *who sadly never made a go of any single thing.*

Terry had the same dream, again and again, in the hospital last year. He'd be coming home from a track meet up the valley, to the motel where he and his dad had been living ever since his mother left. And he would know that the moment was waiting for him when he would walk in and find the body of his father slumped over a note in an unreadable scrawl. He was about to discover how his father had tried to hang himself, in the kitchen doorway, using his Old Marlborough tie. He'd have to look at how the silk had given way in shreds, how his father had crashed down and hit his head on the metal edge of the dinette; how he had not even managed to die the way he intended, because it was the blow that did him in. Yet at the same time Terry would be tramping through the orchard with a hopeful glow lighting up the scene. Penelope Murdoch was about to marry him — in a white dress, furthermore, despite the hurry-up affair. And Terry would be conscious of how he deserved her, in those dreams. He would feel luck between his fingers, like any other currency, and he'd know that he was prepared to work those fingers to the bone to keep it near.

He grabs the pen at last. "My name is Terry Gambril," he gets down, in a wild looping hand.

He has to give a nod to that, give credit where it is due. *My name is Ozymandias....* He can hear his dad declaiming that, of a Sunday morning, while Terry's mother stares out the window at the auto-body shop across the alley and lights another cigarette. *My name is Ozymandias, King of Kings, Look on my Works, ye Mighty, and despair!* Proffering a plate of bacon and fried bread.

That little girl down in the orchard — certainly she's far too young to have been part of the big wave of refugees. It takes Terry back to a better time to see that child. A minute ago she was swinging upside down with her knees hooked over a tree limb. Now someone has given her a pail and she's dragging it around, picking a bit, but talking more — talking mainly to herself. Terry is thinking that he'd forgotten about kids, how every one of them is a kind of perpetual-motion machine. Penelope used to send Jill and William out for him to keep an eye on so she could have an hour or two to do some drawing. How quickly they would get tired of climbing trees, and every other made-up game; then it would be, *Go on with the story, Dad, you promised!* He doesn't want to think of that: how he poured his flawed determination into those stories, how his inventions kept the need to flee contained; how monsters and dragons grew from that, how he held his kids wide-eyed.

He watches the little girl. She has climbed to the third rung of an unused ladder; she jumps off into the grass, and then climbs back and does it all again, and every time she jumps her hair bobs up and down like a shiny upturned bowl.

The two men are having some kind of argument down there. The woman has set up her ladder on the far side of the tree, and when she comes down to empty her pail into the bin she hardly looks at them, or at the girl. Now one of the men — the younger one, who wears a back-turned tractor cap and has a wispy growth of beard — squats beside the child and is telling her something, rapid-fire but keeping his voice low, as if he doesn't want the woman on the other side of the tree to hear. Terry gets a funny feeling in his gut as he watches this. The girl says something in return that makes the man shake his finger in a warning, but he also starts to laugh. He pokes his finger into the soft little mound of her belly before he goes back into the tree. The child wanders away and finds herself a long whiplike twig from the ground. She twirls around and around and the twig makes a high singing sound. She is advancing on some imaginary object, whipping the branch through the air, then springing back, then starting forward again, as if she's taming lions.

Tell us about the dragon, Dad — *tell us how the children got out of the cave!* Yes, he has to admit that he concocted some pretty good adventures involving that dragon, starring a small boy and girl. And when Jill and William got a little older — as the orchard in his care slid into that extended knife-edge phase; as the bank became the living dragon, and Terry's brain was not up to fantasy — at least he made sure they always brought out a bundle of books to read. All those books, still stashed in the toolshed. The nursery rhymes and everything. As if in some happy sunset time he'd be reading to grandkids bouncing on his knee. The lovable old guy who pissed their inheritance away.

He fumbles in the pocket of his shirt for his pack of Camels. He is feeling hungry now, but he's not inclined to go in and eat the bean-curd sandwich, or the pot of cauliflower stew, or whatever Penelope has left for him today. His veins will run with the blood of vegetables, and he will regain his withered faculties and what she chooses to refer to as his spirit. That's what she pretends to hope, anyway. When the husband of her youngest sister had a stroke, the sister sold all her husband's personal things, even his clothes, while he was still in intensive care. "So there you go," Penelope said later. "No wonder he didn't come home again. Nothing to wear."

Maybe it would be wise for Terry to go and pretend to earn his keep — see if Lilian Platt has some errand for him in town. He calls her Lady, to himself. Lady Platt.

Lilian Platt does not like to go to town. She says she has never seen so many fat people in her life, and all of them wearing shorts; all the locals look the same, except for the ethnics, not that she's prejudiced of course. The concrete fence between herself and Gurdan Singh? That merely balances what she's already done on Schmidt's side; and Schmidt was asking for that fence, as Lady is sure you will agree. Imagine launching a lawsuit about her wharf, just because the Schmidts have lived on the lake for thirty years and think they own the view. "As if the lake isn't what the Okanagan is all about, for heaven's sake. Why did we *move* here, if we can't keep our boats and the kids can't waterski? I've brought a lot of money into this town" — popping her bright little eyes — "and if Schmidt doesn't like it" — and her curls are wobbling like those metal things she makes Penelope scrub the pots with — "well, I'll see him in court, and a lot of luck to him."

Lady. He knows he makes her into a cartoon. She may well have redeeming features. Or compelling reasons, at the very least, for having become the way she is. Maybe her parents came to Canada with nothing. Maybe she worked nights and weekends in her father's bakery, and then — despite much shrewdness and get-up-and-go — dropped out of school. And if people are judged just by the results: if in five years these tender acres are covered in pink stucco condominiums, it surely is Terry's fault as much as it is Warren Platt's and hers. Terry doesn't let himself give a pig's whistle, though.

Also, if he goes down there now, Lilian Platt will likely send him back to working on the wharf. With the Sea Ray bumpered just below. The old familiar voice starts whispering again: that cocky kid he used to be, that bright boy, that bad boy, that erratic terror on the basketball floor. *And you still could be a legend, kid! Your wife would be way better off, furthermore.*

Is this how serial killers get drawn in? Some impossible thought crawls close, and maybe you put it aside again and again but it's breathing at you all the time?

The Platt house is peach and teal, with roofs like snowsheds, arched windows two storeys tall; a house so large that Penelope has trouble getting round it in a day. Lilian Platt wears Lycra bicycling shorts around the place, and mostly she works right alongside Penelope — to keep the pace up, probably. Yesterday Terry was repairing a plug on the blender, so he was able to admire the extraordinary chugging motion of her backside as she scrubbed all the copper pots, one by one.

She started in on the subject of immigration once again. These people jabber away in their own language as they pass you on the street, they don't even try to learn, and meanwhile your own kids can't get a proper education with all the

English As a Second Language classes in the schools. So tell me, she enquires, is it right that groups can come in and just think they can completely change established ways of doing things? Take the Hong Kong Chinese, do they ever pool their funds with the local investors? Believe me, Lilian Platt says, this is the sort of thing that Warren knows all about. A capital ghetto, Warren says, is how you might describe the way the Hong Kong money doesn't get around. Also there is, of course, the manner in which they drive.

"Well, but Hong Kong has a very restricted area," Penelope remarked, as mildly as she could. "I don't suppose...."

The roar of Jet Skis drowned her out. The Platt boys had started circling a windsurfer who'd given them the finger when they cut across his path, and they zoomed round and round, making waves the size of tents. Terry had to get out of that kitchen before he did some awful thing. He grabbed his tools and headed down to the wharf.

So then, Christ, there it was! That gleeful terrifying flash, and the Sea Ray tugging on her ropes, bobbing on the waves those stupid boys had made, that gorgeous craft just begging for a chance to do something truly worthy of her beauty and her speed.

He could take her out of there faster than anything you ever saw on "Miami Vice." What a way to do it — carve a canyon up the lake with a thousand horsepower under you. He could jump into that boat quick as the monkey he used to be, and fire her up and head straight for the rocky point. Not till several seconds later would they get the crack of the explosion echoing from all the valley walls.

Come on, Terry, you can even go one better! the well-known voice is whispering at him now, just as after a game, say, in high school, when he would be piloting some hot-wired car along the Summerland road, facing another pair of headlights, and he would never be the one to swerve. *Forget Rattlesnake Point. Let's get creative here. You can do your old neighbour Schmidt one final favour while you're at it.*

Oh, and beautiful this vision is — the Platts all standing there hypnotized as chickens, while Terry circles back and takes a straight run at the boathouse, which will go up like a bomb with all that gas in there. *Jesus, you can take the whole damn wharf out when you go.*

Where is Penelope in this? Terry sees her in the background, rinsing dishes, vaguely troubled, as if she's mislaid a spoon.

◐▬◄◦ ◐▬◄◦

Just to the side of the window of the shack is a scraggy cottonwood tree. The leaves are huge and shaped like hearts. Hearts or spades. They tip and show their silver linings as they turn on the breeze.

It is hard mid-afternoon. The sun beats on the roof. Even the shade beneath the orchard trees will be swimming in the heat, yet those pickers stopped for no more than ten minutes before Terry heard the small echoing thud of cherries dropped into empty pails again, from a tree farther down the hill.

That little girl's name is Lun. He is not sure how you'd spell that. She pronounced it with an almost "oo" sound. Might it actually be Lune? He stopped and talked to her when he went back to the house a while ago to fetch some beers. He always keeps a case or two in the toolshed in the event of emergencies.

It gave him a peculiar challenged feeling, talking to that little girl. He was not sure how much she understood, or even how much he understood in return. "You speak English very well," she told him, though.

She has been here just six months. She is seven years old. She has sixty friends at school — no, a hundred, she decided with a dazzling smile. She had started picking cherries again. Her little pail was perhaps a quarter full.

"So you are having a race with your mother?" That came out sounding even dumber than it had to. *Is that woman your mother?* was what he was trying to find out.

The child looked blank. Terry nodded towards the woman on the nearby ladder.

"Oh, that my uncle wife."

"Is your mother here?" *In the valley? Somewhere near, to look after you?*

"Two uncle here."

"Where were you before?" *So where is your mother,* in other words.

"Ho Chi Minh City," she said. "We escape from there — but long ago."

And then all at once she was acting it out — how she got away in a little boat with seventy people "And the Communists were chasing us, *bam bam bam bam...!*" Her arm sweeping round, imitating automatic weapon fire.

"Then the soldier grabbed me and took me in the monkey house," she said, "and he kept me...!" Terry felt a queasy lurch at this. What was she telling him?

Whatever it was, it was over; the boat went speeding off, and she was on it. Her arm made a straight line, *zoom*, to indicate the speed. "We want Canada...!" she called out, her voice windswept. "Let's go Canada...!" she yelled, then ducked to avoid the gunfire of her former captors, *bam bam bam!*

When he got back to the house, Terry decided to root out something from those boxes in the toolshed, something to occupy the little girl for a while. He found an old Sesame Street pop-up, and on second thought he added a book he had given William long ago, which Terry had always enjoyed reading aloud — way beyond the little girl's comprehension of the language, for sure, but the pictures had always tickled him.

But should he really let it go? A book he'd given to Will? What if it meant nothing to this other child, already stuffed with TV violence? Wasn't there something a little slick about her tale of escape? The voice of Lilian Platt barged into his head, *So desensitized, they're hardly human any more.* What if this child was a tiny con-person, a mini house invader? Today above all things he sought detachment, and look how she had already stolen that away.

By the time Terry was not much older than that child, his father's work had shrunk to the repair of small motors, work that took place on the kitchen table, at home. Terry can still see him sitting there at night, always in a white shirt, the sleeves carefully rolled — an angular man with a fine head of hair, all his outer movements blurred by whisky, yet within the single beam of his concentration his fingers steady on the inner workings of some small machine. Then, with a whistle, Jed Gambril settles back. His elbow knocks his drink to the floor. "Well, she's not going to like that, is she?" he laughs. "Better mop that up, eh, Terry? We don't want your mother to be disgusted, when she finally makes it home. Pour me another and we'll get on with the story then, instead." He is reading his boy Hawthorne's *Tanglewood Tales*. Generally he's passed out cold before he's read a page.

So now Jed Gambril's boy is underneath the table, wrapped in a blanket, riding a white-winged horse while the father snores. The boy hardly looks up when a car stops, a door slams, the car starts up again. The mother comes in, weary but ready for a fight if necessary. She has put fresh lipstick on, making her mouth way bigger than it is. She is straightening her flowered dress, smoothing her pretty reddish hair. She wilts when she sees the same old scene. "You could have put something on the stove," she says. "It's like a barn in here. Come on. Come on out and give me a hug, my little T."

She is going to cry. The boy just keeps his head down and goes on reading.

Terry is not sure how much of the summer afternoon has trailed away. With his final beer, he moved across to one of the shack's old metal bunks, telling himself that if he found a more comfortable position, some helpful thought might sidle up and he could finally write it down. For a while he lay with the book tented on his chest, studying the shreds of tarpaper hanging from the ceiling, recalling how when he was a boy he used to fall asleep with a book peaked over him that way — how that silly kid would turn the light out and feel safe beneath a tent of words. He polished off the bottle, dropped the last of his cigarette inside, listened to the sizzle. It occurred to him, mellow as he had undeservedly become, that this time it might work the other way around — that whatever words he needed might rise up on their own to lodge among the empty pages, and when he looked, in a while, he'd find a fine surprising tale of courage written there. As he drifted off to sleep he could feel himself cut loose, floating on the updraft of those apt persuasive words. Then he was dreaming of water, fire. He woke with a voice in his head saying, *only five cents a pound.*

Earlier, when he gave the little girl the picture books, she looked at him suspiciously. He felt creepy, as if another thing he'd tried to do had become twisted up somehow. If he goes down there now, he will find the pickers all gone home, and the books tossed underneath a tree. That's what gets you in the end — not just big things falling on you but small things, millions, one thing hammering the next.

For a moment he thinks he hears the rattle of rain, but it is only the cottonwood clapping its leaves. Nothing has changed or been resolved, there's just an old guy stretched out on a mouse-turdy bunk with the dregs of the afternoon sloshing all around, and a pen jabbing his ear. A flock of crows is going at it in the pines — no, a murder: a murder of crows — the dry voices scraping back and forth, raising some foolish alarm. The rumble of a tractor reaches him now. The creak of distant ladders, too. He hitches himself up with his back to the wall. He gets a whiff of hospital air. He should not have had those beers. Some bird he's heard a million times and never identified starts giving its persistent head-splitting two-note call.

Then he hears something else. Jesus, he's hearing something strange. He struggles off the bunk and over to the window, charged up by some anger or some fear that has been snaking underneath all day. This is coming from way down in the orchard — a voice that's almost shouting, a small voice, but with an edge. As the wind turns it's muffled. Now it starts up again.

The tops of the trees have sprung into action in the hot sudden wind, whipping a flurry of disguising creaks and whispers over snatches of that sound as it comes and goes. He wrestles with the doorknob. It comes off in his hand. He has to pry the old door open with a stick before he can head out and down the slope, stumbling, groggy, slipping on the flattened grass. Then, slowed by the fear of being foolish, he's sneaking from tree to tree.

It's that little girl. She is sitting cross-legged on the ground, half facing away from him, swaying back and forth.

"...and when she got to the forest where the green men lived," her voice is piping, "they bared their sharp green fangs, and wh-irled their bad green hair..." The book he gave her is open on her knees, and her whole little body gives a hop of concentration, like a Vedic flyer: "...and unc-urled their cr-uel fingernails, and sang their mean songs," — she shakes her finger gleefully — "till Ma-til-da said, YOU ARE ALL OUT OF TUNE...and they fell to their bad green knees and made her Queen."

He stands and listens as she reads the story all the way through, sounding out the hard words. When she comes to the end, she goes back to the beginning again.

HORSESHOE BAY

At Nanaimo, on Sunday morning, Consuelo manages to find herself a seat at the very front of the ferry, where no one can sit facing her. She fills the places on either side with her briefcase, her coat, the still untouched weekend *Sun* and *Globe*. She half closes her eyes, listens to the thrumming of motors as the ferry idles, listens to the sounds of people moving all around her, settling in the seats behind, and in the central section across the aisle. She knows none of them will impinge on her space; there is something formidable about the figure she cuts — the long skinny black-stockinged legs stretched out in front, the peculiar hat pulled almost to the bridge of her nose.

"Good grief," a woman's voice butts in, all the same, from the row of seats behind, "why did you bring *that* up from the car?" Some tall rattling object is being wedged onto the seat back-to-back with hers. Consuelo pictures a birdcage. "Don't let it tip," someone else back there is worrying, "Franny, careful," in a reedy undeveloped tone, "look, you're scaring him."

"Oh for heaven's sake!"

But then a third voice, one that carries motherly care and comfort in every ancient fold, says, "Don't worry, Donny dear."

What a lovely voice. There is a quality so calming and settling in those words. Consuelo feels a lump rise to her throat. She would love to bury her face in some breast and offer up her sins. Still, she resists turning to see who these people are. She had hoped to think as she drove up Vancouver Island from Victoria. That didn't work out. She intends to set about it now. Ever since her husband took a job in Victoria, six months ago, an awful thing has been going on. She flew over there on Friday, expressly to tell Jason about it. Yes, a *thing*. She does not want to give her entanglement with Michael Dreolini the weight of an affair, or garland it in any way. She pictures this thing as a knife she conceals about her person, double-edged and sordid, impossible to keep or throw away. She flew over to tell him, and now she is on her way home and she has not told him after all.

This is Consuelo Robertson, age thirty-one, barrister and solicitor, associate with the Vancouver firm of Bentley, Dreolini and Bragg. Or, as her own mother would put it (with not at all the helpful tones of the dear old woman in the row behind), "But darling, should we not say, Robertson *de Coombes?*" She can see exactly how her mother would say that, intending cruelty for sure, but thinking it so droll. Back when Consuelo phoned to announce that she had married Jason Coombes, ¿*Pero, Coombes que, querida?* had been her mother's half-laughing words. "What kind of a name is *that?*" in other words. She hears again the brittle tapping of her mother's perfect fingernails on the receiver, Morse-coded mother essence. Even across all the miles from Rome to Ottawa, it had threatened to fragment her one more time. For a moment she's right back there in Jason's freezing Ottawa apartment, the snowdrifts humped against the single basement window, the two of them wrapped together in a blanket in his basket chair. ¿*Pero, Coombes que?* Jason had been close enough to catch that, and her rapid-fire reply in Spanish. "What was *that* all about?" he asked when she hung up.

"Oh, well, Mamá likes to trace her lineage back to the first captain general of Guatemala. She wants to know who your mother's family was. I explained how you'd sprung from my forehead fully formed." Consuelo had been preparing to elaborate on that, but he'd started nibbling her ear. He was not impressed with this mother-in-law who, after dumping Consuelo's father — as Consuelo told it, trying to keep this childhood tragedy light — had married some threadbare member of the Italian aristocracy. He didn't care about glitter of any sort. He hardly even noticed what Consuelo wore. He did her the more thrilling courtesy of seeing some deep part of her nature that was not exactly there. So obviously he would be much better off not knowing what the question about his family had implied: how already, sight unseen, the Contessa da Barberino (née Von Muhlen Alvarado-López; formerly Robertson, of course) could picture the man her wrong-headed daughter would choose — a man with no significant family, brilliant but not clever, the sort of man determined to live a life devoted to social justice and remain forever poor. It would not surprise the Contessa in the least, these seven years later (though she herself has journeyed on from contessaship and Rome), to learn how last spring Jason Coombes passed up partnership in a successful Vancouver civil litigation firm, and moved to Victoria to join the government's Native Land Claims negotiating team.

"Now, set me straight please, dear — is that Victoria over there?" This is the kind old-woman voice, from the seat behind. Consuelo can't help smiling at the befuddled question for it has been put in such a wise and helpful tone, as though the old lady believes she is doing her companion a courtesy by getting a nice chat under way.

"No, it's Nanaimo." The ring of a steel trap in that reply. "You wanted to see the Malahat, remember?" This other woman has clearly been stretched to the limit, even this early in the day.

"Oh yes, yes of course," the old lady says. Consuelo imagines her marshalling her thoughts before she tries again. "So we come in at Vancouver, did you say?"

"No." A thin sigh. "There hasn't been a ferry to downtown Vancouver for goodness knows how long. We decided to do the circle route, if you'll recall. We're coming in at Horseshoe Bay."

"Now that will be a treat. It must be years and years since I've been out to Horseshoe Bay."

"Horseshoe Bay is where we catch the ferry to the cottage. We were there two weeks ago, on Labour Day."

Consuelo tries to get comfortable, twists and untwists her legs. She pulls her hat over her eyes. She bought it yesterday when she and Jason were walking around downtown — a Mad-Hatter hat of glazed Italian straw, with a huge yellow rose pinned at the base of the saggy stovepipe crown. It cost a hundred and fifty dollars. She could see Jason undergoing an inner struggle when she tried it on. He wanted to say that paying that much for a hat was obscene when just down the street a homeless man was wavering in circles around his open guitar case, singing a tuneless dirge about how the snakes crawl around. He wanted to say that he had gone along with the entire fit of extravagance she'd waltzed him through the night before — the dinner of pressed duck, the way she insisted they check in at the Empress afterwards instead of going back to the depressing place where he was staying — but that with this hat she had finally gone too far. Then the saddest look came over him, as if he had all at once been hit by the itinerant nature of joy.

This morning, Consuelo drove a dark green rented Lincoln Continental up the island from Victoria. She had torn up the return portion of her helicopter ticket yesterday afternoon, when the airline refused to refund her money after she rented the car. "My mother had a car that felt like this, one of the last of those huge convertibles," she had told Jason when she was driving them back to his apartment, following the ludicrous performance at the airline counter. "Mamá let me drive it all around Port of Spain one summer when I was ten and she was bored. The policemen could only try to smile, because of course we had immunity." Jason's profile was rigid as a totem against the opposite car window. By then he'd clearly had enough, though he still had no idea what was going on.

She wishes she knew herself. It was crazy to decide to go

home by Horseshoe Bay just because the name clanged in her head — as if something lucky and decisive might rub off on her as she passed through. She has no intention of stopping there today. She has to go straight out to the university, bury herself in the Law Library. Tomorrow, for the first time in her career, Andrew Bentley is giving her a chance to argue a major issue in the Court of Appeal.

She was full of this on Friday, when Jason came to meet her flight. She talked on and on about the case, in part to cover up her nervousness. Of course Jason couldn't resist telling her that she is on the wrong side of the law. Taken as a whole, Bentley, Dreolini and Bragg represents the exact opposite of all he believes should flourish in the world. Still, if they remain together long enough to get old, she knows one thing about him. He will never stuff her away — not the way the husband stuffed away the wife in the case of Billings v. Sunnydale Homes.

No sooner had Mr. Billings got his wife nicely disposed of than she disappeared. And then Mr. Billings suffered nervous shock and had a stroke when the management phoned to tell him his wife had been gone for a whole week — adding, *We assumed she was with you.* Andrew Bentley represents the nursing home, of course. And it is up to Consuelo to make sure that the Billings claim does not survive the limitation argument. Just on Friday, he asked her to do some work for him on nervous shock as well. She could be up all night. But that's fine, that's great. She's gathering steam. Though she realizes she has been chewing on a lank end of her hair. Maybe tomorrow she should wear it in a bun? Wouldn't that look more serious and persuasive?

I wish we could bill for all the time the women in this firm spend fiddling with their hair.

She had been at the firm more than a year before Michael Dreolini spoke to her at all. Then one night (she had worked right through dinner with just a bagel and a latté, and she was absently trying to French-braid the straggles out of her eyes) she looked up and saw the source of that comment leaning against the frame of her office door — a long apostrophe in pinstripes, *and his own hair could use some attention, if the truth be told.* She'd heard the articled students whispering about him from time to time, with the secret irreverence that someone so lofty can inspire. The Silver Fox. In the light from the hallway, that greying mane had a lank and tired look. His eyes had a bright, mean glint. Obviously he had decided it might be amusing to see how she'd react.

A tiny bubble of a moment, floating this way and that.

And isn't this what all the fuss is about?

Aren't the people who avoid it actually standing somewhere else, under a different set of stars (and wouldn't they trade places, if they could)?

She said, "Why don't you come and hold this elastic for me, then? If we're into time-and-motion study here."

Michael Dreolini, QC. A man with a fine and jaded mind that leaves her keen and desolate, which may be what she most appreciates in him.

From the seat behind her, Consuelo hears the small sound of a candy-wrapper being torn.

"Here dear — won't you have one?" the old woman kindly asks.

"Are they the kind with Nutrasweet? No, they're not. And you know how careful I have to be."

"But they're so tiny, surely —"

A fluttering breath comes from the old one. The smell of peppermint seeps forward. That cool disguising scent lifts Consuelo across a drift of years. *And never forget, my little one, that you are a child of love!* She is looking down on that love-child, that bewildered little girl, just as when she was five years old and she hovered near the ceiling, looking down on her own small self — the little girl hiding her face in her grandmother's lacy blouse, believing anything she's told, breathing in the smell of dark tobacco, the smell of peppermint to cover up that smell, all overlaid by an energetic French perfume. The smell of intrigue is the smell of that precarious safety, the smell of delighted, ineffectual lies — all through

her childhood, again and again, her darling grandmother telling the tale of the handsome diplomat who cracked apart his
first family (though fortunately not his career) for love of
Consuelo's glorious mother, Eleanora, just a girl herself then,
in her teens.

And you killed him! This is that love-child some years later,
a rebellious teen, just before her mother slaps her face. Her
father's funeral reception is barely over. Consuelo has followed
her mother to the bedroom where already Eleanora has
changed, for travelling, into a white shirt, loafers, two-
hundred-dollar jeans; she has taken off all her makeup; she is
spritzing her face. "So drying," she says, "the planes. You
should take a little care yourself, *querida*. I know, when you
are fifteen you think the beauty will last forever. Or else — as
your expression tells me — you do not care. But believe me,
it matters. And you will come to care. Come here."

Obediently, Consuelo stands like a ninny as her mother
sprays a cloud of moisture in her face. Her beautiful mother
— the haughty Latina features, the ivory skin that is her legacy
from the bankrupt Von Muhlen side. Downstairs at the reception her mother gleamed like a jewel and Consuelo for-
gave everything, indeed she made up her mind that this was
how she too would like to be; she would go and live in Rome
and give up her father's plan for her, which involved Carleton,
then post-graduate work, then maybe even law. She would
follow her mother anywhere. Yet as they stand breath on
breath, her mother's mood abruptly swings. "*Dios!* What a
face — like a little civil servant — so disapproving. Don't make
me have to tell you how like your father you are."

"And you killed him! You destroy them all — first Daddy,
and now even Federico isn't good enough for you...!"

"So there is life in you after all." Then comes the slap. "I
am sorry to do that. But you must learn. Thank God your
grandmother has agreed to stay on with you until you finish
high school, at least. You will find that men are not so easy to
destroy, not unless they get it in their heads to do it to themselves. But we — we must look out as best we can. Because
very soon we will be old." She takes Consuelo's chin in her
hand again. "That is why the beauty is important." Her tone

is strict but almost kind. Suddenly Consuelo wants so badly to hold her mother close. *We are in this together,* she wants to say. *When you are old, you will have me.* But she knows that even then her mother will not particularly want her. *Where do you come from,* pequeña indigna? her mother sometimes used to ask, as if Consuelo's dark colouring and hooded eyes and high curved nose were her daughter's responsibility — leaving out of it completely the blood that ran through the whole of the country where Mamá so proudly traced the generations of her family, *the blood of the women,* as the grandmother loved to whisper, *because* por supuesto *they were all men who came first to take the land and sow the children. Even your great-great-grandfather took as his first wife a beautiful Mayan princess from the north.*

Always that princess. She had to be a princess, of course.

Across from the ferry dock in Nanaimo is an island where great maples grow in a meadow, rounded mounded Rousseau trees with leaves the size of flags. The meadow leads down to a beach, a lonely curve of sand, a tangle of arbutus farther along the shore. On Friday, when Consuelo was prowling around Jason's apartment, she saw, on one of the maps pinned to the wall, that this island was Indian land.

"First Nations," Jason corrected her. She held her tongue. They had just made love. Now they were going out to dinner. It was all like every other weekend when she'd come to visit him, her nerves held taut around the secret that made everything no good — except that an hour ago he had eclipsed that with a betrayal of his own. She was looking at a stranger, a trickster. Already the wildness was starting to build inside her. But "Oh, I beg your pardon, First Nations" was all she said.

The island looks like an enchanted place, she thinks now, foolishly — nothing over there but sunlight playing on the grass, on the tossing branches of the trees. Easy to imagine unseen spirits in the dark of the farther woods. A need for enchantment — for signs — has come over her like thirst since Friday afternoon. She knows she is carrying Jason's child as surely as she has ever known any single thing.

She'd always thought it was just another story of her grandmother's, the idea that a woman could know the very second the sperm made a hit and burrowed in. But as she lay beside Jason on Friday, as she watched light draining from the room, she could feel every cell in her body start to change, tides of hormones, emotions, dark ancestral fears all washing through her. A being smaller than a grape-seed had just lodged inside of her, already printed with the patterning for arms and legs and toes. A tiny brain swimming with murky tad-pole dreams.

When Trish Dallinghouse got pregnant last year, Consuelo had very little trouble giving good advice. They both had friends who were single mothers. Even for those with reason-ably helpful spouses, the reality of children came down to not much more than worry, guilt, exhaustion. It was won-derful how Consuelo had felt no qualm at all telling Trish what she ought to do.

Now she scrunches down in her seat. She is carrying the child of Jason Coombes. This is not her lover's child. Though she is the only person in the world who knows that for sure.

She experiences a peculiar blurring as she thinks this, a queasiness that she cannot put down to morning sickness though she would like to, for this has come and gone for years, this sense that everything owes its reality to its sur-roundings, and is open to change. For a while Jason was her anchor in that swirl. She sees him standing up to make a presentation, in politics class, in grad school — the first time she ever noted him other than as the worst-dressed person in the class. He kept hammering his head while he spoke. It was only afterward that she remembered that. At the time she was completely caught up by his words, by the intensity bouncing around him in waves: he didn't mind at all if oth-ers thought him overboard. "I wish you could have met my father," she told him a few days later. "You are very like him, you know." That was not even remotely true. But how safe she'd felt just then, her little lie fluttering to the feet of his stalwart truthfulness. She imagined how her small deceits might fall like tributes, like a gentle scattering of flowers. Now she sees him waiting for her at the helicopter pad in Victoria on Friday afternoon: no umbrella, his suit-collar turned up against the wind and rain (a greenish suit with reddish flecks; his idea of a Victoria suit?), something deeper than trust in the way he stood rooted there, as if he might be capable of changing her very nature, pulling qualities of goodness right out of the ground.

Yet, as it turns out, she is carrying the child of a man who wants a child so badly that even he would resort to trickery.

Imperceptibly, the ferry has slid out past the headlands. From behind her, Consuelo hears a deep and rhythmic breathing, half whistle, half snore. The old one, of course. From the other comes the brisk clearing of a throat, the rustle of a turning page.

She reaches into her briefcase for her own book. Yesterday she found an 1874 edition of *The Eustace Diamonds* when she and Jason were prowling along Fort Street, not a first edition but a fine one all the same, with a nubbled leather spine.

We will tell the story of Lizzie Greystock from the beginning, but we will not dwell over it at great length, as we might do if we loved her.... She had completely forgotten how the novel started. An absurd tingle steals over her. The ruthless Lizzie Greystock — whose greatest sin, she'd decided when she read it as a girl, was the lapse of courage the heroine had allowed her author to foist on her at the end. But if Consuelo were telling the story of her own life, wouldn't she begin it just that way?

When Michael comes to her apartment on those nights when he tells his wife he is at the gym, he advises Consuelo sternly that she should be over in Victoria with Jason, that McCauley-Watts is looking for someone in Litigation over there, that a word from him would tip the scale — that is, if she doesn't want to go into government like her husband, which she ought to consider seriously, he says.

"You're just afraid I'll tell your wife."

She said that idly, one night about a month ago, but the response was swift. A muscle started twitching at the corner of his jaw. His face sharpened and turned mean before her eyes.

Michael's wife is not his first wife. Above all, he does not want to go through all of that again. But at that moment she saw him come to understand (not from her words, which he discounted, but from something else he recognized, a kind of mirror image possibly) that she would be much harder to disengage from than he had up to then believed. Her stomach clenched, and she had a familiar sense of vertigo. Sometimes when she was skiing she had a similar sensation — when she hovered for a moment at the top of the back wall at Whistler. What if there really were no limits, not for her?

"Don't forget, you're dealing with my mother's daughter now," she heard herself go on.

She had entertained him shamelessly with stories of her family in the months before — her mother, of course, and her grandmother too, who is back in Guatemala City now, in the crumbling old family home, but who calls once a week at least with instructions on the care of hair and skin and fingernails, and on how to manage men. "It didn't come out of the blue, you know," Consuelo had told him, "that take-no-prisoners approach that first rocketed my mom into the world of diplomacy."

Do you know your husband has a girlfriend? Those were the words the wife of the head of the Political Section in Guatemala City had heard thirty years before, on picking up the phone one afternoon. Ten months later, Consuelo was born. By then the injured wife and the teenaged children had long since retrenched to Ottawa.

"And where is she now, the dangerous Eleanora?" Michael had laughed.

"Oh well, she was so much younger than Daddy. She kept up appearances until he was set to retire, but then she decided to give nobility a whirl. Her latest husband is a banker for the Mafia — at least that's what my grandmother likes to suggest. Anyway, she's living in a big pink house outside Miami now." Consuelo's tone had made this all sound like tedious games.

You're just afraid I'll tell your wife. What bullshit. Also, what a degrading and unlikely thing to say. Consuelo had felt like a tightrope walker up to then, high on the tensions of her life, but also somewhat free and clear. She loved the practice of law. The thing with Michael was a hazard, if anything. She had always supposed that he would shed her just like that if she got in the way of what was best for his firm.

Now she looked at Michael lying in her bed, three pillows propped behind him, the sheets all rucked up — a pattern of spring flowers, fifty-fifty cotton/polyester, not at all the sort of linen he was used to in his home, but that added to the fun perhaps for him. She looked at Michael leaning against her bamboo headboard, a glass of Perrier in his hand, for of course he was supposed to be at the gym and so could never drink with her. She could have anything she wanted.

At fifty, like her mother, she could be counting facelifts and the number of lives she'd ruined.

She studied this man in her bed. *I will inform him right this minute that he will not be coming here again.*

The telephone began to ring. Not her phone, but from somewhere inside Michael's discarded clothes. He was going to answer, too. He pulled his long body out of bed, grimacing as if this were going to be his broker, or a client — oh the pressures of his days! It would be the wife, of course, checking that he was truly at the gym. Still, Consuelo liked his body. She liked the way it was nicked and bent a bit from driving too fast and skiing too hard but, like the rest of him, kept trim. His jacket was over the back of a bedside chair. Consuelo reached into the pocket, helpfully. She switched on the phone. *Michael...?* She could picture the wife. She had met her at the Christmas party last year — a woman with amber hair and pale translucent skin, just in her twenties, who, thinking to keep her new husband out of further trouble, had contrived to give him twins. The wife's disembodied voice was like a bat-squeak. *Michael, are you there...?* Michael was signalling for Consuelo to hand the phone to him. She walked out onto the balcony and pitched it as far as she could throw. She imagined that small squeaking voice doing spirals through the air as it fell eleven storeys to the ground. *Michael, you promised to bring home the diapers...the radicchio...the tofu...the gin...!*

"What are you reading, dear?" This is the old lady, rousing herself in the row behind.

From her companion, no reply.

"Do you think we should go and try to find a spot of breakfast?" she suggests, undeterred.

"We had *brunch* while we were waiting in the lineup. Dottie sent us off with a picnic, if you'll remember, to save the fuss of having to line up here with trays."

"Oh yes of course. And those wonderful juicy pickles!"

"The pickles were yesterday."

"Oh no dear, surely...."

"Yesterday at Butchart Gardens, that deli lunch I brought along — corned-beef sandwiches and coleslaw and dills."

"I must say, that was very thoughtful."

A sniff.

"Now tell me" — the quavering tones again — "what are you reading, dear?"

Someone steps hard on Consuelo's toe. She peers out from under the rim of her hat at the passengers milling through the space in front of her. A man in biker leathers struggles with a squirming little girl. A purple diaper bag flops from his elbow; under his arm squints a doll with orange hair. Trish Dallinghouse kept her baby. These days Trish has to carry a breast-pump everywhere, and her cleaning bill for blouses is outrageous, and she has left Bentley, Dreolini and Bragg to take a job with the Law Society, where she at least can rely on regular hours. She can barely afford a nanny, and last week her nanny smashed up her car.

A pair of teenagers takes possession of the forward window of the ferry lounge: a guy with brass from wrist to elbow, half a dozen wing nuts in his ear; a girl in a tattered dress of lace, army boots, bright blue hair. In Japan, Consuelo's lover says, the punks wash the dye out of their hair on Sunday nights and on Monday are interchangeable with all the other salary men and office girls. He says exactly that, office *girls,* waiting to see how she'll react. He went to Japan two weeks ago, on business, taking his wife and the twins. "You should start learning Japanese," he is telling her these days. The firm is thinking of opening an office in Tokyo.

"Now what is that you are reading, dear?"

Of course there's no answer to this persistence. By now Consuelo is more than curious herself. She has a vested interest in what people are reading. Michael maintains that books are finished. In ten years, he assures her, books will be relics of a dinosaur world. Now that he truly understands how this annoys her, he goes on and on in that vein.

In Jason's apartment in Victoria, books and papers are stacked on every horizontal surface. Still, what a rootless place it is. He is living in a suite in a tower halfway between the Court House and the Empress, the furniture covered in brownish glassy stuff. Apart from a five-foot pile of newspapers by the door, the only contribution he has made to the decor is to tack up maps of the disputed Chiefly States: the thousands of acres claimed by the Lheit-lit'en; the offshore isles of Haida Gwaii; the vast territory that was the ancestral home of the Gitksan and the Wet'suwet'en; the lands of the Musqueam, the Carrier-Sekani, the Tzeachten — names Jason rolls into speech like lines of epic poetry.

He believes so strongly in First Nations causes that he forgets who he's working for. She fears for him, in fact. Recently he managed to influence senior civil servants to commitments that caused an uproar when they leaked. She suspects he is likely to turn into a fall guy for the government, if the negotiations go sour. He could do with a wife more devoted, less sleazy. She hates the part of herself that wants to duck and run.

Sometimes, though, it can make her spine tingle to listen to him talk. He defies logic, really. "Look around you," he will tell her; "Is the present madness built on logic? Well then, my god, it's time we started thinking differently." Sometimes he can carry her along, carry her back through smog and noise and urban clutter to a fine and mythical time where — sometimes — she wishes she could stay. For maybe he is right. Maybe goodness will win through. Maybe it doesn't even matter if it wins through or not, as long as a person lives in a certain way.

When she got to his apartment on Friday, it was late afternoon. The rain had stopped. Clouds above the harbour bloomed with gold against a ragged sky. They stood together at the window for a moment, looking out, and Jason took her hand. "Connie, I hate this," he said.

"Me being here?"

"Your having to go again. Why do we live this way?"

"You know why we live this way." She was safe from any argument on this. It was essential to his vision of himself that her work be as important as his.

But shouldn't she try to look after him a little more? He ate too much and worked too hard and never had time to exercise. He was getting almost pudgy, but she was selfish in this as in everything. What she needed from him was the sense of safety, the rhythms she trusted — oh, and a sense of being on the bright side of the world for a change. His hair was very short and wiry and he washed it every morning with something that made it smell humble and excessively clean. Michael Dreolini's hair was musky. She did not want the smells of Michael Dreolini's body crowding into this moment when her husband was leading her to bed. Soon enough, he would know. She could feel the secrets preparing to leak out and stain her skin.

She breathed in the smell of Jason, the rising warmth. *Oh, but listen. I am doing this for you. I will arm you with the bitter potion of discouragement, the way the mythical Jason was armed by Medea.* She ran her hands over his face, she kissed his eyes. She traced the surfaces of his body as if she had never touched them before. So poignant, the bodies of men. She watched his face sadly, with tenderness so acute it brought her to the pitch — just the awareness of how vulnerable he was. And then he gasped and shuddered underneath her. And then he fell asleep immediately, escaping in that way she had forgotten, that slamming of a door.

And he had not worn a condom. How could they both

have neglected to notice such a thing?

And he twitched and smiled, locked behind a wall of deep unconsciousness.

"What did you say you were reading, dear?"

Consuelo hears the squeak of lips that tighten, then finally relent. "It is about China during the Boxer Rebellion. It's called *The Seeds of Time.*"

"Oh, lovely — a novel, then."

"No, of course it's not a novel. It deals with the effect of the foreign incursion on that structured Confucian society."

"You must find it very interesting."

"Yes."

"Ah, but tell me...." The old lady pauses, gives herself time to get her thoughts in a row. "Have you been to China often, Frances dear?"

"As often as you have. Those times when Philip was posted there."

Consuelo decides to turn and fix that horrid woman with a stare. But "Oh yes, we were so lucky, weren't we," the old lady is saying mildly now, her voice full of happy recall. She might just have opened a drawer and come upon a lovely lace-wrapped gift from long ago. "I feel so fortunate," she adds, "to have had those lovely trips."

Consuelo stands, pushes her hat back, peers out the window, scratches her neck, then turns and looks directly at the row behind. The reading woman — Frances — is so like her voice that Consuelo feels a momentary flip. All this has happened before. She fumbles through her mind, trying to find the door that opened and then closed. Of course déjà vu is just a case of scrambled synapses. Is this what pregnancy does? Frances has brown hair pulled straight back, then elaborately looped and twisted, hair much younger than her face, but the face is in no way giving in. Expensive clothes. A dark silk dress printed with a pattern of gold chains. She is a case of determined self-absorption, Frances. She sits wonderfully upright, frowning, tucking in her chin as she turns a page. The other woman is a good deal older than Consuelo had imagined. The old lady is slumped sideways now, eyes closed, giving an impression of long lines of crumpledness: hair that has faded through grey; furrowed skin; yellowish shapeless tweedy clothes; and that crumbling face sliding sideways towards the reading Frances and then jerking up again. But as Consuelo stares, the old woman opens one red-brown eye and takes her in.

And someone else has her under observation; a man seated next to the old woman, on the aisle, is staring at Consuelo steadily, and not with pleasure, out of the unmistakable face of an ageing Down Syndrome child.

She sits down, flustered. She hears a rustling, a laboured sound like wind stirring damp piled leaves, and the old lady clears her throat. "Pull up your socks, dear," she says. Out of the corner of her eye, Consuelo sees the young-old man bend and fiddle with his socks, obediently. He wears a smart blazer with a crest, grey flannels, a very proper shirt and tie. "I think I've got them on wrong," he says.

"Oh well dear, just pull them up the best you can. That's all right, Donny. You can change them when you get home." Her voice holds so much love.

"Oh good, here's Philip!" All at once Donny is leaning forward, lifting his coat off the seat across from him, hurriedly shuffling things around. "You can sit here, Philip!" His voice is eager, transparently glad to have Philip appear.

Philip. Who spent all those years in China.

It could almost be Michael Dreolini standing in the aisle. The same silver hair, the same height, even the same pale blue cashmere pullover. Can it be that there are only so many types in the world? Or is it simply that this one is lodged so deep within her brain that even when she's ninety a similar form will flash before her, a reminder of something she once either lost or stole?

Oh, but he's a ramrod, Philip. None of that slouching which so deceptively brings Michael down to the level of others, that eye so quick to check out weakness here and there. Philip allows these members of his family — for surely this is a family group — a slim percentage of a smile. "No no, I'll just find a place over here." Before there can be a word of protest, he has broached the line of seats across the way, sidling past knees balancing sandwiches and coffee cups and trays, until he reaches an empty seat right in the middle of the row. He folds himself down as neatly as a jackknife, and leans his head back and closes his eyes.

"He's tired," Frances says. "He's done all that driving, after all."

"Oh yes, yes indeed. That was a long drive we had. Where is this boat heading, by the way? Do we come in at Vancouver harbour, did you say?"

"No." As if she's answered this a hundred times, not twice. Perhaps she has. "Horseshoe Bay."

A brother and a sister and a mother. And Donny is the third child, who, with the vast power of the helpless, has made the family what it is — the mother's love poured into him, poured and poured, leaving Philip and Frances to grow up rigid with the guilt of being normal, a disability that no one else could ever see.

"You could just put us on the bus, then," the old lady says. "When we get to the other side."

"Don't be silly, Mummy. I left my car at your place. Philip will drive all of us there, and then go back to the hotel."

"I don't want him to get too tired. You could just put us on the bus, you know, when we get to the other side. We are coming in downtown, didn't you say?"

Now Consuelo thinks she can feel the beam of Donny's gaze, focused not so much on something ahead as on concentrating his own interior energies. The sister casts a pall over him, probably. Over the old lady, too. Probably when Frances is not around, the old lady can think just fine.

Consuelo pulls her hat down again, allows herself to be lulled by the throb of the great engines of the boat. *Where are we going? Horseshoe Bay.* She pictures the house where the old lady lives with her son, who has always lived with her — some huge old place on the edge of Shaughnessy, with leaded windows, peeling steps, someone who comes once a week to do the lawns, which get smaller and smaller all the same, overgrown by bushes, year by year. They have their dinners in the den, the mother and the son. They have a comfortable routine from which they've roused themselves for this outing — yes, it's been lovely, but they are quite content all the same, staying home. Consuelo wishes that this crossing of the strait could be prolonged and prolonged, that she could travel back and forth, on and on, considering the lives of others, the tips of lives, hints of problems she will never be called upon to solve.

Soon she will go out onto the deck, when the ferry approaches land. She will stand at the stern. She will feel the freshness of the wind. Maybe it will lift the hat right off her head, and she will watch that jaunty stovepipe bobbing in the wake as the ferry rounds the sugarloaf hill at the entrance to the bay.

"What about Chinese food tonight?" the old woman stirs herself to say.

"I told you. Philip and I are going out."

"Oh dear me, yes of course. Well maybe I can take you out tomorrow night, then."

"Tomorrow Philip is flying back. That was all arranged months ago."

"What a pity. We'll miss him, won't we, dear?"

A blast of the ship's horn rattles the windows. The boat is rounding the tip of Bowen Island; they don't have far to go. Consuelo would like to turn and say something to her companions of this voyage. *It has been a privilege*, she might begin. They will look startled, then quickly turn away. *Don't think I think it is easy, either,* she will add, to Frances; *You are truly awful, but you are managing it quite well*. Frances will not take this as a compliment, but Consuelo understands the sacrifice required to keep yourself so precisely at the centre of your world.

"Well, I believe I will just go and find the toilet," Frances says to her mother. And no sooner is she out of earshot than *FISH AND CHIPS!* a small and strident half-human voice announces from directly behind.

"He's getting restless," Donny says. "He's tired of being in the dark."

"Don't take the cover off, dear. We'll soon be home."

Yes, exactly as Consuelo imagined; as soon as Frances leaves, conversation flowers. What a nice trip, the mother and son agree; how lovely to spend time with Philip. Oh, and how enjoyable it was, staying at the house of the cousins by the sea. "I worry about the winters for them, though," the mother says. "That sea wind."

"I liked taking their dog for a walk," Donny says. "I thought I was lost once, but the dog knew where to go." How companionable they are. "Franny and Philip are going out to dinner with friends tonight," Donny tells his mother now. "Out by the university." Clearly he does his best to keep on top of everything. Perhaps the mother and the son are absolutely, happily balanced at last.

"I don't think I want to go out to McDonald's tonight," he says.

"No, dear? Would you rather stay home?"

"Oh yes. Yes I would. After all this travelling around."

"Well, what would you like to eat?"

"Bacon and eggs!" he says, with quick happy decisiveness.

"Oh, that would be lovely and simple," the mother says.

A MESSAGE FOR MR. LAZARUS

FRIDAY

This is about Wolf Lehmann, a man whose life I like to believe I changed. I met him only briefly, that time at Punta Verde. He did not thank me for my help. Indeed, I could tell by every line of his body — the way he sat rigid in his chair like a little rock, dreaming flight — that he accused me of trapping him into giving up his tale. But he was a sophisticated man. He did not think that I had also in some way taken hold of his soul. *Because my soul is beneath significance,* he might have said. *In any case,* he might have added, unable to help glancing around for an audience that was not there, would never be there again, but still governed his way of talking, even what circled through his brain, *aren't we just imagining some frilly lampshade we pop on our heads at the last minute, hoping to pass in the masquerade?*

He did not fool me, however. I could see how he yearned.

And when I tell his story to myself now, some years later (I have been confined to my bed these last months, with little to do but run through the events of my life, which turn out to be lamentably few), I like to imagine all of it — all of it — from his point of view. The skin of the man he loved slides over my skin, and I suffer loss as he did, pain, humiliation, guilt and fear. And when the boy trembles in my arms, I breathe in the smell of that innocence, and even I become confused.

I can't help it; I put on that small man's life and flee to the remote southwestern shore of Costa Rica, and once again it is Good Friday, and the year is 1987.

At Punta Verde, the Pacific coastline makes a dramatic twist. The jungled hills lie to the north; the sea is to the south. East and west run rocky headlands strung together by crescent after crescent of palm-fringed golden sand. Long ago, a tribe of Indians had a hilltop fortress here: *Eighty-four hexagonal buildings, linked together like cells of honeycomb,* was how the conquistador Juan Vásquez de Coronado described it in a letter to the King of Spain, *with roofs of straw, but tall as spires, held up by beams two fathoms round.* This tribe was one of the fiercest on the coast. And when the Spaniards made an offer of salvation, the Indians of Punta Verde declined. They fought until they were overrun, until the last man was killed.

Centuries later two women from Vancouver built a small hotel on the same spot. El Más Hermoso was the name they chose. Most Beautiful, that means. Or most perfect, one might say — as in (muttered through explosions of cigar smoke, at the common table of the Vancouver Club), *I hear Irene Lansdowne has found the perfect place to make her getaway.*

That was some time ago, of course. Scandals succeed one another quickly, leaving smaller ripples than those involved can ever quite believe. But in the meantime, Irene Lansdowne and her partner have managed to establish an almost first-class small retreat at Punta Verde. Several publications — though not yet *Gourmet* — have written up the place, and El Más Hermoso has been successful at attracting a semi-toney international clientele. If there are still rumours, season after season — well, speculation has only given the hotel an extra, gilded, wavering dimension for those who like to come here year after year.

For a time Wolf Lehmann was one of those. He came here often, always with the same companion. Today, after an absence of several years, he sits on the shaded terrace alone.

Several people have noted Wolf Lehmann's arrival on the terrace. A slim blonde woman from Denmark returns her attention to her companion's knee. On that touchingly scarred athletic surface (scarred long ago, for he is an investment banker now) she has just written *rosin boller,* which means raisin buns. This is the first day of their secret holiday, and she is writing the names of all the sweet things she can think of on his knee, with a slim, unvarnished but well-tended index fingernail.

At a table a little distance away — by the railing, where there is a fine view down to the lower terrace and the pool — a crab-coloured American wearing reflector jogging shoes is keeping a close eye on several recumbent, slowly turning figures in bikinis. Down there, also, three men in desert shirts — men whose faces have taken on a lean and battled look from the hard conditions met in watering holes on the edge of the Nicaraguan war — are talking loudly from bar stools beneath a coconut-fringed roof at the far end of the pool. The lovely faces never turn in that direction. The women reach into Gucci bags for lotions, flip the pages of ¡Hola!, accept a fruit juice from a passing waiter now and then. These gleaming women are from San José, down to spend the Easter weekend by the sea. Their husbands, though they may be elsewhere often, are observing the family nature of the holiday by being here with them today. There are no children in the pool. This is not the sort of place for that.

In the shade of the upper terrace where Wolf Lehmann sits — which is where the meals are served — an extremely large woman and her even larger husband (wearing a linen suit from Barnum and Bailey, Wolf thinks, with a pang, for there is no one here to tell that to) are studying the menu with extremely close attention.

But did Wolf hear a laugh when he sat down? This is like an inner tic. All his life, he has heard laughter around hidden corners, whether or not it is real. *Humiliation lives in the pit of the stomach. Its juice is always in your veins.* That annoying, meaningless phrase was circling in his head as he drove from Playa de Coco. *Yes its juice is always in your veins....* He believes this must have been what distracted him not far from Garabito, so that he did not have time to avoid the snake that was stretched right across the road.

Wolf Lehmann is a small bald man. He is tanned well beyond the current cautious norm, his head shiny, oiled, fastidiously shaved. He wears well-pressed chinos, sockless loafers, a *guayabera* he bought in Playa de Coco at a beach shack run by Nicaraguans, maybe Contras, maybe genuine refugees. A boy called Manuel did the bargaining for him. Wolf is not here to think about the boy. *(But if you can stay until the rains,* señor, *even the fence posts will make roots, they will put out little vines....)* No, he does not need to think about the boy, nor does he intend to dwell on the matter of the snake. It is about the *guayabera* that he is uncomfortable now. He dresses with the care, the attention to detail, of those who suspect that, no matter what, they will always miss the mark somehow. Perhaps when Irene Lansdowne comes out to greet him after her siesta she will read something into his wearing of this garment, something mistaken but sly. He should have left the ruffled shirts to the Americans, the ones who hired the boy's cousin's other boat and went out far past the islands after swordfish.

Playa de Coco is near the Nicaraguan border, and Wolf has driven that whole distance in not much more than a morning. He is hungry. *Famished, actually,* he tells himself. He has been waiting quite some time for his club sandwich to arrive. He keeps nodding off to sleep, then jerking up again. And every time he does that — lets his guard down — he is back in his BMW once again, screaming across the plain of Guanacaste, refusing to be passed even on blind corners, which is how they drive here, everything dry, smoke-hazed, the mountains in the east shimmering like dreams; and flame trees are flashing by, and herds of thin white cattle, and now and then a palm, and in every little village he has to slow for pageants of the Crucifixion, and the roads are crowded with groups of adults, children, dogs.... Then suddenly something is on the highway, right in his path, *something slides out, alive and wild,* and instead of jamming on the brakes, he hits the gas instead.

He jerks awake to find a boy setting down the glass of soda water he also ordered quite some time ago.

"*¿Por favor, dónde es mi sandwichito?*" he asks.

"Your sandwich, club, is coming in one moment," the boy replies. But once he has walked off to take another order — at a measured pace that gives a clear message of how pre-occupied and purposeful he is — Wolf sees that someone has put ice in his drink. He twirls the cubes around in his glass, tries to absorb that cooling sound, for of course he will not drink this. But neither will he make a fuss, call the boy back again.

Ah, but look at this, this is what I came for, isn't it? For ever since last night (he tells himself) there has been just one thought in his head: arriving here, settling on this covered terrace where the hot sweet air blows all around, where you feel your very essence start to melt in the cubed shade, the fountain splashing in the courtyard, the sea wind washing over pink wooden chairs and tables, flame-coloured bougain-villea, the red tiled roofs of the cabanas on the slope below, and all these colours throbbing against the colour of the sea. Look how the purple drops off to stony green beyond the reef, a green that sharpens, becomes a blue so extreme it could slit the heart of anyone who let it. Wolf is drifting off to sleep again. He sees a jade knife he was offered once, in his place of business, in Toronto — Mayan, he declared to the man who brought it in; no doubt smuggled out of the Yucatán. He gave the owner of the knife the name of a man he knew in Rosedale, who was less fastidious about dealing in contraband. The knife had brownish stains lodged in the scrollwork of the grip, a beautiful and eerie thing. Wolf sees that jagged wedge of stone ripping through the tight fabric of the sea.

Yesterday afternoon, when Wolf called from Playa de Coco to make his reservation, he got Irene's partner, Maddy Wilkes, on the phone, *for which,* he said, *thank God.* She sounded amazed to hear from him at all, and who could blame her — even more surprised to hear where he was. Then, to ice the cake, "Now, Ja, Maddy..." (slipping back into half-German, the way he still, after all these years, sometimes does when he is rattled), "I wonder, also, if you would book me in under the name of...Lazarus, if you would be so kind as to indulge a whim. Yes, Charles Lazarus." Simply picking a name out of the air. That one strikes him as particularly unfortunate now. He had been thinking of Emma Lazarus, perhaps, whose words on the base of the Statue of Liberty (too often repeated to little Wolf by an American, briefly a protector of his mother) had later been influential in persuading him to emigrate to Canada instead.

Still, Maddy had laughed. "But of course, my dear."

My, how Wolf looked forward, yesterday, to seeing Maddy Wilkes again. He has not seen her for — he tries to figure it out — it must be more or less four years. And it has been three weeks since he left Toronto, three weeks since he has seen a single soul who has the least idea who he is. The anonymity of travel can become a burden eventually. You begin by thinking it will be restful to slip in and out of rooms without having to keep up any sort of face; but what it comes down to is every day having to reinvent yourself.

And even back home in Toronto, it had been a great deal longer than three weeks since Wolf had spoken with anyone he thought he could call a friend.

But really. Charles Lazarus. He feels like clutching his forehead. The made-up name is a dismally foolish complication of an already tricky scene. He can't help picturing what his companion of so many years would have made of that — how, if André had got hold of this example of Wolf's foolishness, he would have repeated it again and again. *So un-Wolf-like*, André would tell people, *who we must admit, for all his faults, is not an underhanded sort of guy. Something I've had to take him to task for more than once, I hate to say.*

So un-Wolf-like? Yes, he allows that; unlike him right up until sometime yesterday, perhaps. Unlike him no matter what Maddy and Irene may be thinking now, if they have been in touch with people from Toronto (as they must have; the reality of this strikes Wolf fully for the first time). Undoubtedly they've had visitors, regulars, who believe they know exactly what happened with himself and André. He thinks back to his conversation with Maddy yesterday. Certainly there was surprise in her tone. But something more?

Right to this minute he has let himself believe that he will be treated as the select one here, just as he and André together always were: not merely given the best table, the best cabana, even the honour of buying after-dinner whiskies for Maddy and Irene, but gathered in as a needy friend. He realizes that all along the road, as he drove, he was picturing how Maddy would welcome him, how, despite all her duties, she would take time to give an old friend an hour of tea and sympathy. Hadn't they always hit it off? She *was* an old friend, wasn't she? And surely, of all people in the world, Maddy and Irene would not be the ones to shy away from him now.

Wolf has heard that there is not one jot of truth to the rumour that when Irene Lansdowne discovered her husband was having an affair, she stormed into the Vancouver Club (this was well before women were allowed into the dining room for lunch) and marched up to the common table — where he was eating the Friday fishcakes in the company of a senator, a university president and a judge of the Court of Appeal — winged him with a crescent-shaped vegetable dish, then stormed out without a word. That story has been denied by all of those who might have backed it up. Irene must have started it herself. On the other hand, it is the absolute and certain knowledge of people from Vancouver, or who have friends who know people from Vancouver, that Maddy Wilkes was a dancer once; no, not ballet, heavens, look at the height of her; exotic. The kind who dance in bars. Or hadn't she been some sort of minor beauty queen? Before she became the secretary of Norman Lansdowne? No, not Norman, Hugh — not the land developer, the lumber one. There was an episode, in any case. It took place at the Oak Bay Beach Hotel. Irene Lansdowne followed her husband one weekend when he had declared that he would be off in Ottawa. She burst into the room. She dumped out all the bureau drawers. She emptied her lighter over a hill of elaborate lingerie.

As luck would have it, the girlfriend was wearing not one incendiary item at the time. So Maddy was still unsinged when she began her life anew in Costa Rica, with Irene.

There were other, milder explanations of how the partnership was formed. But Wolf has never considered himself much wiser than the rest; André was the one who loved rumour. *Oh, just call me a saint,* he used to say, *I make things true by belief and repetition.* He loved to spin proof from a tangle of absurd details.

Now Wolf is heavy with the need to sleep, so where the hell is his sandwich? Across the terrace, that huge woman in a flowered caftan has had a second bowl of nachos in the time that Wolf has waited — *good heavens, barnlike would be too delicate a word for her.* The man with her is reading through some sort of typescript, making notes in the margin. *And now she's feeding tortilla chips to that equally gargantuan man. Whenever she wants to attract his attention she slaps him on the knee. A couple. Set in their awful couple ways.* For more than a dozen years, Wolf's every sentence has gone through several loops of laboured replay, just like this, and he is aware that this attempt at catty observation has not made the grade. Almost in the corner of his vision, the ever-present person who is elsewhere lifts an eyebrow, looks away.

A boy is bringing the fat woman and her husband drinks topped with umbrellas. She takes the umbrella and sticks it into the top of her pouffed-up iron-grey hair, like a tiny Chinese hat. Her husband, without a word, reaches across and removes it, collapses it, sets it on her paper napkin. She has been smiling, and she continues to smile. She lifts her glass and clinks his, though he seems to repress a shudder, as if she's done that once too often in their lives. Then — perhaps to change the direction of his thoughts — she makes some comment, and Wolf finds them both looking his way.

Are they wondering why he's sitting here without being served? Does he look as silly as he feels? He has not succeeded in regaining the attention of the waiter, who has slipped through the beaded curtain that leads to the kitchen.

When Wolf was driving here he was picturing the basket of fruit that would be waiting in his room. Surely its absence must be the merest oversight, he hopes. Always, when he arrived before, there would be a basket of mangoes and papayas and small bananas with pinkish skins, a Gauguin-like arrangement done by Maddy, set out on the table on the balcony — and chilled bottles of gin and vermouth, so that by dinner André would be in another of those extreme and treacherous moods.

André. *Oh Jesus fucking Christ,* Wolf hears himself say, which is not the way he talks, he never talks that way, *why can't you get out of my head and fucking leave me alone?*

André is dying in Toronto. He is blind now. Chemotherapy has stripped him of almost all his hair. It is two years since he developed full-blown AIDS. And his lover has swanned off to Costa Rica — that is what Wolf's present hosts must surely have been thinking when he called. Wolf believed that he had no more bitter lessons to learn, but suddenly, for the first time, he understands something more. All his friends, all of them, worldwide, are not his friends at all. They have all just accepted him, because they love André. What can he have been imagining, coming here? Except that he has nowhere else he can think of, now, to go.

Oh yes, it's true that Irene and Maddy will not shy away and ignore his outstretched hand, as others have, in Toronto. They won't keep aside his cups and spoons and sterilize them. Will they?

They will just think that he's a monster and a turncoat.

And they don't know the half of it.

Palm leaves rattle in the wind. Voices float from the pool. A scarlet bird flits by, a flash of colour so particular it slits the surface he has carefully held tight, sucks him down, farther down, into a crack so small he has assured himself he need never look at it again. The mother of the boy at Playa de Coco wears a bright red dress. She sits by the door, facing a garden of carefully arranged stones fenced in by a hedge of thorns. The father is asleep in the hammock.

So you are going to the islands, is all the mother says. *Manuelito, take care.*

When Wolf reopens his eyes, the scene has changed. An unusual cloud has covered the sun and the whole stretch of water between the headlands has taken on a surface like luminous green stone. Yes, jade. That stone of mystical qualities. In ancient China, it was placed in royal tombs. Jade has fallen to earth from heaven; having it around ensures immortality. Something like that. It has been years since Wolf made his study — quite exhaustive at the time — of jade artifacts of various cultures, especially those of Middle America. But a sudden interest in the subject was one of the indirect reasons he first found himself here at Punta Verde, with André.

He'd had a client, a strange obsessive man, who wanted to get hold of what he called an axe-god. He showed Wolf photographs of objects in the National Museum in San José. Wolf had seen such things before, but had never paid much attention. The stone effigies known as axe-gods were a variation on a functional forest-clearing tool, but made of that rare, beautiful (life-ensuring) and most durable of stones. They were powerful religious objects, yet none of the scholars understood what role they had played. The upper portions of these highly sharpened jades were carved into representations somewhat human, somewhat birdlike.

This man who came to Wolf did not want a facsimile, he wanted a true original, unearthed from some tomb or ruined temple, Mayan, or Olmec — many fine examples of the work of these cultures had been unearthed from Costa Rican sites — or from the region of Nicoya, which produced a large proportion of this species of carved jade. The provenance was all the same to him, as long as the piece was rare and genuine, which would make it contraband. This was some time after the Mayan knife had come to Wolf and he had sent the seller on his way. He had not kept the number of that man. Anyway, a plain ceremonial knife, even if once used for human sacrifice, was not what this other chap was looking for. He wanted someone with connections and a sleazy way of doing things to find him an axe-god. It never ceased to amaze Wolf how the urge to possess the most unlikely objects came upon people. Fortunately for him.

Wolf sent the man off, politely. He said he would let him

know if such an object ever came along. And then, as has been the way with Wolf all his life, he became intrigued. He had no intention of trying to search out cultural treasures for his client. All the same, the question led into an area he did not know as much about as he would have liked. He began a detailed study of jade artifacts. And one of the things that lured him to this country, when he and André first started talking of coming here, was the idea of visiting important collections of pre-Columbian art; so that when they did come, he arranged to spend the initial days in San José.

They had left Toronto in a blizzard, and they arrived in San José in the dark. It was not until next morning that they felt the attraction of the place. The hotel was built around a tropical garden with a large pool at the centre. André slid open the door of their room. A small tile patio lay outside. A trellis of bougainvillea shimmered in sunlight so caressing that Wolf felt a complete new being stir within, not that northern creature curled up against the cold but something rapidly expanding, like those paper seeds you can drop into water and watch grow into flowers before your eyes.

"I'm not going anywhere," André said. "You can meet all the experts you want to. I'm not budging from that pool."

Wolf was more confident of himself, in those early days with André. "I'll give you a morning," he said. "But then you really must come with me, at least to the museum. For one thing, some of these jade figures remind me a great deal of the work you have been doing. You'll be interested."

So he dragged André around to all the places he had written ahead and made arrangements to see. They went to the museum, and the Instituto de Seguros, and they were shown through the collections of pre-Columbian art at the Central Bank of Costa Rica. Professor Jimenez-Ortez was kind enough to spend some hours with them, as well. The jade came to intrigue Wolf. André was more taken with the gold.

Many times, after that, Wolf was tricked into expounding on the subject of pre-Columbian art. Yes, tricked is how he puts it, because as he sees it now he was set up — not consciously, not by any one malicious person, just by the idle indifferent hands of the fates — to believe that his expertise could make a jolly contribution to the occasional gathering. He held forth to Irene Lansdowne on the subject, for example, the first evening they were here, when he and André were invited over to her table for an after-dinner drink. That time, though, Wolf quickly gathered that he should let the subject go.

This was hard. Because imagine his surprise, earlier that day when they checked in, to walk into the lobby of El Más Hermoso and find a wide glass case in which — cleverly lit so the contents seemed to glow from within — thirteen jade effigies lay. Axe-gods. These were even more astonishing examples than he had seen in the museums of San José. The largest figure in the case was perhaps nine inches long, carved from the most prized of all the jades, a deep blue-green. The upper portion portrayed a bird, probably a quetzal, with a high feathered crest. The wings were folded in on either side of the long pointed beak, in a way that suggested enormous curbed power. The lower half of this figure — of all of them, indeed, whether they had bird faces or faces with a severe and rather sinister human look — consisted of a smooth knife-sharp blade.

Could these possibly be genuine? They would be worth a fortune, in that case.

"Oh for heaven's sake," Irene Lansdowne said that evening. "No, but I'm not surprised you were taken in. The Ticos are getting wonderful with fakes. Or 'genuine reproductions,' as they like to say. Of course, I was offered them as genuinely genuine — all very hush hush, you know. That was back before we even built here. The word got around that we had money, I suppose. Some little German with a sneaky lemur face came up to me in the lobby of the hotel up the coast where we were staying.... Oh I beg your pardon, Mr. Lehmann. But there are still some of the bad sort knocking around the world, as I'm sure you know — and of course the Latin countries attract them like flies."

When that sort of thing happens to Wolf — as it often has over the years — the first wave of shame he feels is for the person who has made the careless or hurtful remark. If he can cover it up immediately, perhaps it will be almost unsaid, and this will be a courtesy. "Ah, but the art of this country," he began, "it has such a feeling, doesn't it? Objects so small but with such power. As if the power has lurked within for all these centuries, waiting to seep out and influence our lives."

"Oh my," Irene Lansdowne said, "now there's a thought." That eyebrow. The way she could let you know immediately what a fool you were.

"My friend is wonderfully perceptive," André said. "Not only that, he knows the words to the whole of 'Alice's Restaurant.'"

Those jade carvings are still in the lobby. Wolf looked at them anew when he checked in today. He has never resolved the question of what their provenance might be. He is not convinced that they are fakes. Laugh as you like at the obviousness of the observation, they do give off an extraordinary sense of power. When he looked at them today, he thought perhaps they represented whatever force it is that lies in wait — and it can wait a long long time, he knows that now — to cut a person down to a size even smaller than you believed you were before.

Yes, *Gourmet* is a publication that consistently eludes Irene. Also *Condé Nast Traveler*, and even *Destinations*. With this in mind, she has established a regimen that puts demands upon the guests as well as the staff, at least as far as dinner goes. Perhaps this is what is holding up Wolf's sandwich, for he can hear plenty of activity in the kitchen.

At dinner, as he recalls, course will follow course, an evening's entertainment, each dish dictated by what is freshest in the morning market. That is the pronounced philosophy; Wolf knows that haughtiness and ample garnish sometimes help to disguise a lesser reality. But he has never minded if the fish is oversauced to cover up its bony nature, or if there is nothing much at all within the puff-paste swans — nor have the other guests, it seems. "Style, it is all about style — look at them, they love to be whipped into shape in the interests of rubbing shoulders with famous lesser lights," André used to say. "Look, there is X; see how he's lingering by Irene's table, hoping to be asked to join her, just because Y was here two weeks ago. Doesn't that sound deliciously louche, referring to those poor old dodderers as X and Y? If only they knew! But it's us, Wolfman, the favoured guests are us or no one. No one else will be invited to share her after-dinner brandy all the time we are here — which proves my point: with style you can accomplish anything!"

Wolf and André came here seven times. Once they even stayed a month. And it was true, Irene was taken immediately, that first time, by André's talent — though that was the only visit when André was able to work. There was a gazebo by the pool in those days. A group of local musicians played there in the evenings. André sketched there every morning; at least for the first few days he did that, before everything went sour, before he began sleeping in until almost the afternoon.

"Well, Charles Lazarus, my old friend!"

Wolf gives his head a shake, blinks several times, a pantomime though unplanned. "Irene, Irene...!" He feels his accent about to thicken, as trepidation turns him into a German once again.

"Well — what a treat to see you. It's a bitch, though." This through a stream of Gauloise smoke. "Living's a cruel and bitchy business, isn't it?" She pulls out a chair and folds down sideways and stretches her long legs. She is wearing Bermuda shorts and a dark green cotton muscle shirt. Smoke seeps up in rivulets, following well-worn channels in her face. In the years since Wolf has seen her, her blunt-cut hair has turned wiry and grey. Before, she had a stark glamour — eyes rimmed with black, the flat chest of her T-shirts freighted, in the evenings, with bibs of pre-Columbian-looking gold. Now her only ornament is a platinum Rolex. André would say that she looks awful, a consolation in a way.

Charles. How is he going to get out of this now? And she loves it. She will never let it go. Better not to say a thing, he thinks. With luck she'll get tired of it, or make a slip and restore his proper name. He was being absurdly cautious yesterday. What possible danger could he be in — well, from that source, anyway? He has to admit that he is glad to settle in here behind a scrim of anonymity, but of course he did not mean it for his friends.

"So — how long have you been down here?" She picks a shred of tobacco from her tongue. "Maddy said you called to book from *Playa de Coco*? Imagine leaving it to chance like that! Charles, Charles — that's not your way. And you know we're absolutely chock-a-block all season now. Isn't it lucky we had a cancellation? I had a qualm, of course, about giving you that same cabana."

"It's fine. Your arrangements are perfect, Irene."

"Well, that's undoubtedly the grandest one on the sea-view side. And somehow I assumed...." She bends and starts picking at her heel. *That you weren't coming here alone*, is the thing she wants to say.

"My, but you look absolutely splendid." She straightens up, takes in the shirt. "I like that *campesino* effect." She ruffles her fingers through the air, then settles back, bites her thumb. "You're certainly full of surprises. It's wonderful to see you taking everything so well."

Bitch. Though he hates to think that way, even when every tenet of his life has proved to be mistaken, most especially what he believed himself to be. Bitch. What can she hope to know, her eyes making him smaller and smaller, *that little German*, she says.

She shifts a hip, takes out her pack, taps another Gauloise into shape. "And how was the drive? The roads must be murder. All those little Ticos running to the sea. You're very brave, Charles." Lifting an eyebrow that displays her regard.

"Ah yes indeed. The roads were extreme. And, actually...I had a most unsettling experience on the way...!" For he remembers all at once how André would arrive anywhere on such a wake of controlled disaster, how people loved that — how people would draw him in and laugh and comfort him.

"Just before Garabito, I ran over a bloody great snake," Wolf says. "Yes, yes," he persists, "first I saw a hump-backed creature — an iguana I suppose — come scuttling out onto the pavement. And then, like an arrow, the snake in hot pursuit. I swear it stretched right across the road."

"And you ran over it."

"Well, it was too late, of course, to slow down. It was quite horrible. It felt like running over a fat firehose."

"But you went back, naturally. To make sure it was out of its misery."

He does not want to begin to consider how she might mean this. Momentarily it does not matter, anyway. He is fleeing across the plain of Guanacaste once again, and he sees the snake, and he runs over it, and everything dims.

"Well well, what an adventure," Irene is saying. "Though perhaps there is an alternate point of view."

"Ah, but the extraordinary thing" — Wolf has to admire how his voice carries on — "the remarkable coincidence is that when I stopped at Garabito I saw that same snake — well, at least that is what I allowed myself to fancy — that same creature, skinned and flattened on the wall behind the bar. It was wider than the track of a heavy-duty tire."

"Two snakes in a row." Irene shifts her gaze out to sea. "So you'll be looking for the third one, I dare say."

Wolf would like to laugh; if he were wearing a hat he would like to throw it right into the sky, as his mother did at Wiesbaden when her last lover left her years ago. For a moment he sees that flowered circle of straw rising into the air. Imagine that he pictured finding sympathy and solace here.

He listens to the clink of dishes in the kitchen. He hears the thud of a French knife. This sounds like Maddy, the emphatic thud of a person who has far too much to do. Irene has always been hugely frugal, and help is hard to hold, so Maddy struggles by as best she can. Why did this seem delightful to Wolf before? What if it's nothing but a kind of slavery? He remembers how sometimes he helped her out in there. He helped her make *cioppino* once, another time Charlotte Russe. They laughed, you could almost say they larked about, until Irene made one of her entrances.

"So, well then, how is he?" Yes, and here she is, closing in finally. "I mean, of course, André."

That voice is ruined by smoke. And what right has she to this moral high ground, anyway? *How is he managing,* is what she means, *while you, you little shit, are down here getting up to God knows what? No, please don't tell me. I certainly do not want to know.*

Wolf has composed some helpful lines for this moment. For no one truly wants to know the truth of how André is — not *that* reality. *Everybody in the clinic says André is an inspiration, Irene* — that part is true, amazingly. *Indeed, it's beautiful you know* — *he wears his death as if it were a cloak of all his talent, all he never quite fulfilled...!*

"He's...doing not badly, Irene."

"Under the circumstances, I suppose you mean."

She is getting pleasure watching him squirm. She would like to force him to describe everything to her.

Across the terrace, the fat woman in the flowered caftan has been served a banana split complete with cherries and what looks like shaving cream. Wouldn't it be just Wolf's luck to have his sandwich finally arrive? To have to endure Irene's scrutiny as he tried to eat or pushed the food away?

Maddy has started singing in the kitchen — some trills that flutter wildly up and down the scale, then crash into an old Beatles tune. Irene catches the eye of a waiter hovering near. Without a word the boy slips through the beaded kitchen entrance, and the singing stops in the middle of a phrase.

Well, but perhaps they have finished with the topic of André. Perhaps Irene will leave it mercifully there. After all, I am a paying guest, Wolf thinks.

I am a small man, I am no one really, he had planned to say to Maddy. He had seen himself in the kitchen wielding a knife as he said this, his voice with a pleasant ironic tone. *I have mostly tried to live an honourable life, but in the wings. What implacable human weakness makes that sensible aim impossible?*

The boy returns from the kitchen and stands in pointed silence by the table. This boy is black, true black, not a hint of Spanish or of Indian in his features, not a hint of the coppery sheen of the boy from Playa de Coco. *Manuel.* This boy is from Limón, on the Caribbean coast. Nelson is his name.

"My goodness," Wolf says, a little late, "let me buy you a drink, Irene. Is it still Glenlivet?" She shrugs. Nelson goes to the bar and pours a double. A boy far from home, but smart. He thinks he knows everything. He thinks he knows exactly who this man, Charles Lazarus, is.

Irene shakes out another cigarette, and Wolf is swifter now. He takes out a lighter he carries just for others, a slim gold oblong bearing the crest of a duchy of a lesser Hapsburg line, a griffin and a serpent entwined. His mother, when she made a show of using it, always smiled a mysterious smile that hinted at some grand affair. In fact Wolf was with her when she found it. This was when there was still enough money to trail around the European spas. They were walking along the lakefront at Stresa when in a flowerbed his mother spied a glint of gold. She was wearing a careful copy of a Dior New Look dress. He still remembers the sad and useless way her rayon skirt spread on the ground.

"Now if I'd known I was coming," Wolf is saying, "I'd have brought cigarettes."

"Oh that's all right. Walterson was here, he's kept me going for a while." Irene's voice has a slick of purpose on it now. "He was back in Toronto, just before." Walterson, a man of many khaki pockets, another of those covering the Nicaraguan war. "That's how I heard. Of course when he was back there he spent time with André. What he says is that it won't be long. But that's not news, I'm sure. He also said he didn't know where you had got to. Apparently someone else was there. At the hospital, I mean. So he didn't want to ask."

"Irene, it's complicated."

"Sure. No sweat. Believe me, I understand. So anyway, you are a man of leisure now."

"We sold the business, yes. I sold the business. But that was a while ago. In fact, André and I have not...had any dealings for some time."

"Ah Wolf, Wolf, don't be so defensive. It's just sad."

She puts a hand on his arm, actually reaches out and touches him, gives him back his name. And now Wolf truly regrets the meanness of spirit he has allowed to take hold. He searches for something he can say that is generous and right. But suddenly Nelson is at his side, setting down the sandwich. Also, unrequested, he has brought a second double scotch. Nelson's shirt and shorts are blinding white. He never smiles.

"Oh, my." Irene hands him her empty glass to take away.

"Nelson, you'll go far.

"He's good," she says, when the boy has gone. "I work them, these boys, but they know when they're well off. I take care of them." She is looking hard at Wolf. "So the situation is — I don't need complications. I'm sure you know what I mean. I have to live here, Wolf. And things are very different than they were in the carefree days."

You would hardly know he has been hit. Any rush of confusion, anger — yes anger, which is making the pink chairs and tables pulse in and out like fishes, something he may remember in later years if he is allowed them or may never think of again — is covered by the extra armour of his Playa de Coco tan. Irene reads him all the same. He avoids her eyes. He removes the toothpick that spears the pickle to his sandwich. The toothpick flies a small Canadian flag.

"Oh come on, " she is saying, "don't take offence. I know how fastidious you are. We used to feel so sorry for you. Maddy didn't see how you could stand it. So I want you to know something." The hand returns to his arm. "We don't blame you, Wolf. In the end we all have to look after ourselves, wouldn't you say?"

Wolf is sitting on the edge of his bed. Beyond the balcony there is darkness now. From far below comes the sound of the sea. The tropical night took over while Wolf believed he was not even sleeping, while he was thinking this could be a rehearsal for eternity, this waiting out the remaining afternoon, beneath a fan, alone on a king-size bed locked away in air so thick with heat it was like breathing under water.

He has swallowed two tablespoons of a special Romanian compound containing mystery ingredients said to keep the Ceauescus young. The empty spoon holds a reflection of the fan, which whirls tiny and complete in the silver hollow, beneath a greenish film. He sees himself in there too, his head a foolish egg-shaped thing. If he strikes the right position he can create a halo for this egg, out of the slow-turning blades of the fan.

Maddy didn't see how you could stand it.

Ah, but that is precisely the point, he replies to Irene now.

We were assailed with arrows from all sides — these words flash into his head — *it was necessary to put the torch to the entire village, therefore.* So spoke the Spaniard in his letter to the king. Those buildings, like cells of honeycomb with roofs of straw, but tall as spires. Wolf sees how they burst into flame. He smells the burning flesh, he hears the cries.

It was not from a travel book that Wolf first learned of Punta Verde, nor when he was doing his research on the jade, but from a rare volume he came across, one of the lucky finds of his life, he thought then. Yet he might have forgotten the story of that doomed tribe had it not been for the breath of fate one day — so that later, when André's friends began to talk to him of Punta Verde, the decision to come here seemed lit by a flare of synchronicity.

He had found himself driving north to the Muskokas the very weekend after he first met André, to the cottage of the parents of friends of someone André knew. It was so unlike Wolf to go off like that, to subject himself to the whims of strangers who might have dreadful taste in music, anything. He felt brittle, too — the ache in all his bones of André's body on him, hard and hot as a train. The farms and fields and trees beside the road had an electric clarity, everything portentous, brightly edged, the way things look before a migraine or a storm.

All at once he was wheeling off the highway and up a mean rutted drive, at the bidding of a cardboard sign nailed to a pole. *Trust me, I have a nose for this*, a feel for this, he said. And marvellously, minutes later — in an old stone farmhouse, in a room where the air smelled of mildew and neglect, in a pile of tattered books — he came upon a rare translation of the chronicles of Gonzales Fernández de Oviedo, "Historiographer of the Indies," its leather binding hardly scuffed. The letter to the King of Spain was on the very page the book fell open to. Wolf studied this, expecting that André would admire his skill and luck at such a find. But as he read, the horrid picture took hold: *In each house lived five and twenty men, with wives and children*, Vasquez informed the king, *at least two hundred souls. As we were assailed with arrows from all sides, it was necessary to put the torch to the entire village, therefore. Yet this warlike tribe gave evidence of having been a long time settled there. On the slopes down to the sea they had cut away the jungle to grow flowers.*

Ah, look how the Spaniard makes particular note of that, Wolf thought, *how the natives had cut away the jungle to grow flowers.* He glanced around for André, hoping somehow, with that passage, to convey what he never could say on his own. He would give the book to this lovely young man, a precious gift but more than that, a signature, a seal. He pictured how they would bend together over the volume, André's indrawn breath as Wolf presented it.

André was flipping through a stack of paintings done perhaps by someone's aunt. He was wrinkling his nose. He pulled out a foundering ship at sea. "Stuff like this could be contagious," he said. "I'm going out to get some air, I feel my blue period coming on."

Wolf had to smile, of course; how could he help it? Yet in that moment he saw what he would forget again and again. He forced himself to remain in that musty old house, if only to put off conceding that his friend had total power. And so it happened that the copy of Oviedo was not the end of his luck for that day. He was sorting vaguely through the paintings where André had stood a moment before, then through the clutter in behind, when he came upon something tall and wrapped in burlap. This turned out to be a single section of a Muromachi screen.

DOGGED BY LUCK...! That runs through Wolf's brain in bright red letters. Where do these things come from? Earlier this afternoon, after Irene left him on the terrace, he was imagining her wished-for spread in some glossy travel magazine, picturing that very scene with himself in the background, thankfully a little out of focus, a man trailed by the hot breath of mongrel fortune.

He wipes the spoon carefully. It is one of the few pieces his mother did not sell. He pours himself some soda water, swallows an Antabuse tablet as he does at this time every day, though he probably has not needed this for years. He goes over to the mirror, pats his cheeks, feels his flesh.

Walterson was there. He said he didn't know where you had got to. He didn't like to ask, because someone else was there.

The bathroom of Wolf's suite contains a tropical garden along one wall. A frog lives in that garden. At first Wolf thought it was an ornament — creamy green, a little smaller than a chicken. During his shower, he looked up and saw it spread-eagled just below the ceiling, concentrating all its energy on staying there.

You have been dead, you delightful Wolfman. That was André, kneeling over him the very first night, years ago. *Now I am going to teach you every sort of sadness that being alive can bring.* A person's life can change just like that, everything lost, discarded, offered up willingly. It turns out we are so ripe for being shattered, so desperate to feel.

He pulls shut the outer door of his room, locks it, checks it, starts along the breezeway, then turns back and checks the door again.

Lights glimmer in the trees around the pool, and dissolve and reappear through the layers of perfumed air. Cicadas sing. Wolf walks along the path, turning over and over in his pocket the slim gold lighter. Even tonight, he may bring it forth, snap someone's cigarette alive. "Ah yes," he may say, "indeed, there is quite a tale...."

He pauses at the bar. All his life he has hated going in to dine alone, entering a room full of laughing groups and couples. In the mirror behind the bar, he can study the guests out on the terrace. The tables are covered with white linen, and all is elegant.

Well, so Wolfman — who would you most hate to be locked up in a train with?

André, André. When he chose he could be such diverting company.

Wake up, Wolf, who have we got here tonight? We will have to make sure Nelson doesn't seat us near those three-hundred-pounders. It's so eerie, isn't it, the way fat people breathe? André always hated silence, unless he created it himself. *But look at those golden people over there, those Danes. Is that love, do you suppose?*

Have you ever seen two people quite so glum? And they've left their spouses eating plükfisk *in Copenhagen, wouldn't you say?*

Wolf can study himself perched on a bar stool studying the other guests. He can study the sleek bald head, the blue-striped shirt, the red loafers without socks. The scene is striking in a way. He thinks what Dali might have done, or maybe Bosch: the palms, the moisture-haloed lights, the tropical Easter banquet scene, and in the foreground a little betrayer in red loafers — still worrying that he looks foolish going in to eat alone; *still with a carrot up his ass,* he hears his former lover say.

His gaze collides with one of André's three-hundred-pounders, the woman who was feeding her husband guacamole this afternoon. Tonight she's wearing fifteen yards of red and purple. She is fussing with a flower in her hair.

So who does Wolf end up in a very small compartment with? Well, absolutely — your friend with a hibiscus in her hair. And she's onto you, Wolf. She's a woman of voracious appetite, and food alone won't do it. She has spied the cracks in your soul. Still, as luck would have it, her husband is the author of uplifting novels, based upon the Bible. You can tell by the suit. Crumpled like that you just don't buy, you either have it or you don't. So here's the deal — just you and her, the Simplon Express. Twelve and a half hours....

At least she'd have a picnic, Wolf butts in. It wouldn't be so bad. She'd have partridge and caviar.

She wouldn't share, though.

Oh yes she would. She wants to be liked.

Oh Jesus, oh God — well don't encourage her!

Wolf looks away. He looks at the moon falling on the water, some lights moving far down the shore where he knows there is no road, only jungle, only sand and bush and trees. He looks away. Not like André — for having trashed these people, André would suddenly reach out and they would open up like flowers, revealing hidden qualities like homes in foreign countries where they insisted you should stay. Wolf peeks at the couple again. In the night air the hibiscus in the woman's hair has clamped shut and protrudes above her ear like a horn. But she gets no clue of this from the man in creased white linen. Tonight perhaps he simply does not see her, having looked at that same face for years. He taps his fingers on the cloth with an air of vexed importance, and glances around at everything but her, while she talks and talks and smiles and smiles.

Waiters move, not too quickly, carrying trays of gorgeous fruit-filled drinks, wine in buckets, glasses clustered like bouquets. Wolf finds himself looking a small curled fish in the eye. This is followed by a thimbleful of sherbet, then a single chop of veal wearing a frill. It is not until dessert that the incident occurs. The man in the rumpled suit asks for more. He and his wife have consumed a bottle and a half of rosé. He puts out an arm and stops a waiter in his tracks and commands, "Bring the Dobos torte around again, my friend." Not even attempting the Spanish tongue. And he must indeed be someone, for the torte comes round.

Maddy herself comes out to serve. She cuts generous slices from a complete and pristine cake on a silver tray the waiter holds. She is wearing a long tunic of brownish cloth like tree bark. She has become a column the same width from top to toe. All that Wolf can recognize of her former beauty is her hair. *Of course she was a beauty queen — you can tell by the trapped look.* That was André, the first time they were here. *Everything downhill from one completely trivial day, yet she's condemned to go on brushing her hair — though I expect there was a moment when she thought Irene could break the spell for her.*

How beautiful he was, Wolf's lover, then. He was wearing a cream linen shirt that Wolf had bought him for the trip, a fullish Russian-looking shirt with a narrow stand-up collar, before that look became the thing. They had stopped at Playa de Jacó for a day on the way down, and André's gaunt intensity was glowing from the sun. And it was going to be fine, Wolf thought that night. This was early in their time together, a month after André had come into his life, or not much more. Though Wolf had showered, the smell of that demanding body opposite was still upon his skin, and even if it was not going to be fine, that night he did not care.

Perhaps she thought Irene could break the spell for her.... All those years, he was able to take Wolf's breath away with how he saw things, when he chose, when he emerged from the gloom which, more and more, Wolf was held accountable for.

Wolf raises a hand, hoping to catch Maddy's eye. He converts this gesture into a sweep across the forehead.

Maddy looks at no one. She moves with lethal submissiveness. Irene, sitting by herself as always, watches her.

The large religious writer and his wife pick up their forks again. At a nearby table, the Danes dip their fine long noses into the vapours of their brandy and wave away dessert, close to tears.

"Coffee by the pool, *señor?*"

"Oh...! I beg your pardon. My thoughts were far away."

This is a young fellow Wolf has not yet talked to, a boy with clear Indian features and proud calm eyes. Wolf produces a nice smile. "What is your name?" he says.

What is your name?

"I am Rodrigo, *señor.*"

I am Rodrigo, I am Alberto, I am Kurt, I am Ron....

Wolf sees a waiter's uncomplicated face; he sees André's eyes go hooded, abstracted, as if pondering higher matters Wolf would never understand — grumpy too, determined and rude, for whatever followed would turn out to be Wolf's fault, no matter which way he moved.

"Then you would like a little whisky, maybe," this Rodrigo says.

"Ah, thank you, Rodrigo. Thank God, no. It would seem at the moment I do not need a thing."

"Wolf! Wolfschen...!" That whispered voice throws him for a moment, as he starts back towards his cabana along the dimly lighted path. *Mutti...?* he almost whispers in reply. For his mother, against his will, has walked into his thoughts quite often lately — daintily, ineptly, with her tragic selfish smile.

It is Maddy. Yes, she did call him Wolfschen sometimes,

in the old days, in a fond and teasing way. She knew how the diminutive annoyed him. And because of that — because the knowledge referred back to things he'd told her that he had told no one else in the world — he didn't mind it from her, it cemented a secret bond.

Yes it's Maddy, in the shadow of the breezeway, standing still as a column. With the weight she has gained, all her features seem to have enlarged proportionately, and as he comes close he has the impression of a South Sea island carving standing there, but done in marble, the broad white nose, the heavy chin. Without a word she puts her arms around him, and the spongy crinkle-fabric texture of her bosom swamps his face, and he is breathing in the oniony vanilla smell of her. And as always, though he has been longing for some welcoming touch, he has to restrain himself from backing off too quickly. *I am so selfish, he is thinking. I can never give to anyone who needs me.* For look how Maddy is shivering. She is frightened. Something is truly wrong. Yet Wolf's first thought, before decency (and curiosity) takes over, is that he doesn't need this, that he has enough troubles of his own, that he would like to be safely, quietly, quickly back in his solitary state, in his room.

"Ach, but Maddy sweetheart," he is saying. "Whatever is it? Come with me and have a drink. I have — well, you know me; I have some soda water. Or shall we go back to the bar?"

"No, no, Wolf!" She is whispering still. "No, listen — I can't talk now. But tomorrow? Can I meet you by the pool? At noon?"

"Yes, of course. Or should we go for a drive?"

"No no. I can't be away. But Irene is going over to Quetal for lunch. That lawyer from Vancouver, who has the house up above Las Espuelas? Well, there's some sort of deal she's talking to him about. I don't know what it is. She's gone all mysterious."

"Is that what's worrying you?"

"No, no, Wolf. No, but...."

"Maddy, you're terrified."

"I'm fine."

"Look — do you need money? Do you need to get away?

I don't have a great deal on me right this minute, but I could give you five hundred. Or better yet, I could drive you to San José. We could leave immediately."

Maddy is laughing, despite the state she's in. "Oh Wolf, you're really something."

"No, but seriously, my dear...." He doesn't know why he is doing this. It is not in any way what he wants to do. And once again he sees himself as ridiculous, taking her distress like a terrier and shaking it and shaking it, way beyond what she needs.

"I just need to talk to you," she says. "I'm so sorry I didn't come out when you arrived, but things were a bit...out of control just then. You know? And now, I have to get back. But tomorrow? Promise?" She bends and brushes her lips against his cheek, then hikes her long brown narrow skirt up and runs down the path that leads around below the pool and back to the hotel. When she turns he catches the flash of her heels, and sees that her feet are bare.

Wolf makes his way through his darkened room and out onto the balcony. He sits down with a feeling of relief, yet at the same time disappointment, in one of the deep cushioned wicker chairs. He could be on his way to San José right now, carrying an old friend on some rescue mission that would give purpose to his squalid little life. They could be bumping in the dark up the Puriscal road, headlights veering wildly, the red earth of some washed-out hillside flaring up before them signalling sudden danger, or strange yellow eyes gleaming for a moment as they rounded some sharp corner. No lights along that road. Miles and miles of what is called dry jungle between the small sleeping settlements, and the road climbing steeply all the way to the central plateau. That is the fastest way to San José, that is the way he'd pick for a midnight getaway.

But Maddy and Irene have had another domestic fight, that is all. Irene is turning into a monster, possibly. Though it takes two to play that game.

How she toyed with him this afternoon, when he told

her about the snake. *So you went back, naturally. To make sure it was out of its misery.* Thinking that concept so perfect, so absurd, given his flight from Toronto. She knows nothing, Wolf thinks. Not even what she thinks she knows.

Yet he saw the snake and he ran over it. He didn't even try to slow.

"*¿Qué es el nombre de eso?*" he asked the dark-eyed waiter, shortly after, at the Garabito stop — not so much to get the name of what he'd killed as to contain the shock of seeing it again.

The café was open on three sides. Photos of prize bulls hung on the pillars, bulls of the local type, with deep loose throats and sloped-back horns. All along the wall above the bar stretched that flayed and flattened skin, diamond-patterned, grey and black, with dots of yellow where the diamonds met along the spine.

The waiter looked him up and down and shrugged. "*Serpiente,*" he said. He turned abruptly, carried a platter of small black clams to a nearby table: a noisy group from San José. Gold watches, glittering chains, designer bags hung over chairs.

Wolf sipped his soda water, a blameless drink. He had a familiar feeling of peering through a slit at something, a sense of some great truth just beyond the edge of what he could see. For a moment everything he had done and everything he had failed to do appeared to be contained within the circle of this occurrence, *two snakes in a row,* which had surely shaken him.

The roadside bar was full of families heading to the sea for Holy Week. He found himself watching a sleek large man, the one who had just been handed the platter of clams. This fellow was digging in, eyebrows raised, face alive with satisfaction, not at all bothered by a woman tracing patterns on his arm with a long red fingernail. "*Ah pobrecito,*" the woman laughed, "I absolutely forbid it, my king...!" and the man broke up at whatever this was about, and the holy medals in the V of his white shirt shivered together with a purely delighted sound. All the others at that table were laughing too, and Wolf observed their round-eyed faces, the laughter which was all the same not simple, which allowed for several sides to everything.

Wolf had never felt so alone. Yet alone was what he wanted to be. Nothing good that he could think of had come from any single connection in his life; how could he possibly imagine that it would be fun — fun! how could he even be thinking about fun? — to go across and join those carefree-looking people, share the laughter, buy them drinks, join them in eating *chicharrones*, a platter of which had just arrived, crackling deep-fried pork rind; just the sight of that would have been enough to give his dear Mutti a heart attack.

Nor did he want to hear the boy's voice. He had hit that snake because he heard the boy's voice. Was this going to go on and on and on? He was sorry about the holy medals on that fat man's chest, which reminded him of a story — so that he had to see the absolute and shining faith in the boy's eyes one more time.

Every year a pilgrimage took place to the cathedral in Cartago, Manuel had told him. Thousands walked up into the central plateau from the farthest corners of the country, in the hottest wettest month, and many of them walked the last mile on their knees. Last year Manuel's cousin had walked all the way from Playa de Coco, and he had seen people from even the richest families walking the last mile on their knees.

Wolf tried to picture the people at the nearby table taking part in such a pilgrimage. That sort of Technicolor faith had always rather given him the creeps, yet for a moment he felt surrounded by a kind of tinselled goodness that might almost be accessible.

Then, immediately, *Holy Jesus — tinselled goodness?* a too-familiar voice was exclaiming, right in his ear. Exactly as if André had sidled onto the seat next to him, changing the very shape of Wolf's thoughts, as always, without the least thought that he might have any stake in his own point of view. *Oh come on Wolfman! I don't mind you making friends, but don't give me any talk about faith. This attack of conscience is getting to be a frigging bore.*

When he left Toronto, Wolf did not care where he went. It felt like vast inertia drawing him to retrace steps he had taken with André, in the place in the world where he had felt the most intense emotion, high and low — as if agony wore a coat, summer and winter, in Toronto, but so did happiness, simplicity. Maybe he had hoped to see a point where once he could have gone a different way; or some milepost, relating not to his unsure terrifying future — for he could not bring himself to look ahead to that — but to where he had been.

Never did he expect any transforming gift of luck to come of this, least of all an out-and-out miracle. He would have laughed at such a thought. Yet some such thing occurred. Something inner as much as outer. He held, for a few days, the most fragile and incandescent truth in his hands.

Now Wolf sits on his balcony listening to small fitful rustling noises in the jungled slopes below, watching the slow movement of the mist-drenched stars. *Thank God I do not need a thing,* he had said to that young waiter. Ah, Jesus. Why must every rustle in the dark remind him of some fervent episode? If we could root out need completely, how simple and clear the universe would be. If streams could slip gently to the ocean, if planets could sweep round in their orbits, without the need of gravity.

You don't take whisky, señor? *You don't take rum? What shall I bring then for our picnic, a few little beers? I can get them from my uncle at the cantina. I help him sometimes. He will let me have them free.*

I don't drink, Manuel. I am a person who can't drink.

Then my mother will like you very much. My father he drinks all the time. He spends all the money, even what I earn when he can get it. He is either angry or he sleeps.

A boy like that should get away. A boy like that would come to no good working at a hotel where only coarse types come to fish, and throw around their cash, and assume: *Well it's just Central America.*

A week ago, Wolf said that. Seven days is all it takes to make and unmake a world.

All last night at Playa de Coco, he had paced his room, returning again and again to the balcony as if some breath of courage or at least determination might settle on him. He had watched the moon slide across the sky. The moon was red, inflamed, enormous. The hills across the bay were black even in the day — burned off by angry fleeing Nicaraguans, the boy had said when he had brought Wolf his breakfast that first morning, just seven days before. Such a graceful boy even in the oversized starched jacket. A mild presence. Yet he turned back quite fiercely at Wolf's idle question about the fires. "Do you think we do that to ourselves, *señor*? No no. Before the Sandinistas, here in Guanacaste we did not even lock our doors." *(But if you can stay until the rains, señor, even the fence posts will make roots, they will put out little vines....)*

Last night Wolf had already packed his bags, as "Of course I will not do this," he had said. "Despicable," he had said, as he waited till all the local staff had gone before he went to the office to pay his bill. Oh yes, he had left handsome gratuities in various sealed envelopes. He had paced his room.

A tree that he could not identify leaned across the corner of his balcony, each leaf composed of ten sets of smaller leaves along the stem, and at the tip a single one. He counted leaf after leaf and could find no variation. The leaves rustled one upon another against the paler black night sky; pattern on pattern emerged from this, each different, made by shifts of air. Wasn't it possible to think that things were ordered, that each variation had a root in mathematical certainty? Wasn't it possible that, in the infinity of natural regulation, any single action of any man could sink like a stone?

⊙━‹‐ ⊙━‹‐

SATURDAY

Wolf Lehmann was born in Berlin, in the suburb of Frohnau, in a house designed by his father, a student of Walter Gropius and Miës van der Rohe.

The father's practice began well, but Günter Lehmann's (totally selfish, his wife said) continued association with the Bauhaus school, in the years just before the Nazis came to power, threatened all that he had achieved, not to mention the security of his young family. When Hitler closed the school in 1933, Günter might have found himself in a difficult situation if his young wife, Leni, hadn't caught an important eye. After that, she became more than ever resistant to her husband's desire to move his family to America, as so many of his colleagues had. And perhaps Wolf's father was not a very strong man — *but God knows,* Wolf has often thought, *I am not the one to judge these things!* In any case, the family stayed in Berlin and Günter was involved in the design of some minor public buildings, and "Uncle Hansel" became a frequent visitor to the household. Indeed, one of Wolf's earliest memories has him sitting on Uncle Hansel's knee, a pale-eyed face peering into his with feigned goodwill, through wire-rimmed spectacles, as little Wolf pulls the *Gruppenführer's* hair. Hans Von Schlichting was a senior official in the Propaganda Ministry, which might explain why Günter Lehmann managed to go on getting work — for along with his unfortunate modernist bent, he was one-quarter Jewish. As it was, Günter and his children (Wolf had two older sisters) became part of that statistical group whose dangerous lineage was conveniently erased, and when the war came Günter was offered a commission. He found himself dispatched first to the desert, then to the Russian front. So that, unfortunately, Uncle Hansel is the closest thing to a father figure that Wolf can recall.

None of this is to the point. The point is that Wolf's earliest memories take place in that glass and metal house his father designed, where form met function perfectly. In that house were many objects that barely fitted, yet were beautiful indeed. His mother came from what she liked to call an *aristocratic* Dresden family (the second "a" prolonged into several syllables) — manufacturers of porcelain. People who, for generations, had been extremely fond of lovely things. Leni had inherited her great-grandfather's collection of oriental pottery, for a start; and carpets, and saddlebags, and cloisonné stirrups that might have belonged to Genghis Khan, and three whole sets of Meissen, and a cabinet of Japanese netsuke, and a pair of candlesticks her great-great-grandmother was said to have been given by Napoleon. Wolf was a lonely boy, looked after mainly by a nanny. His sisters were away at school, his mother was busy with the war effort, as she called it (though she doted on her son, and cuddled him outrageously, whenever she had the time). But even after Wolf was old enough to go to school himself, the thing he liked best — the safe place he made in his life — was befriending these quiet beautiful objects that filled his house, coming to know them in every small detail. How could he explain it? It was a passion, *completely loony,* as he said to André years later. (But by then, it was obvious that this obscure passion had turned out to be worthwhile.)

After the war, after the Russians had come through and then receded, he began haunting the libraries and the newly reopened museums. His father escaped from prison camp in the east and arrived home a total stranger. Like Ulysses, Wolf has often thought; except that this Penelope had not been tending to her weaving. Leni had made a conquest of an American colonel. She had a way with Americans: her giddy shrewdness, her Old World charm.

She refused to part with Wolf, but she was relieved to have Wolf's two sisters taken off by Günter to a more respectable life in Bonn, where reconstruction planning was going on. Rosel and Lisi had become large, sulky, incommunicative girls in any case, she said, and they ate so much that she could hardly afford to keep them, *Gott im Himmel,* she'd already had to sell the Meissen and her pearls.

After Mutti sold the house and they finally left Berlin, Wolf went to work for Bernheimer's in Munich, the most prestigious antique dealer in the land, where even Goering had once shopped. Everything bought and sold in that baroque palace-like establishment was of museum quality. Wolf had no need to go to university, or study formally. But by the time he and Mutti emigrated to Toronto, he knew enough, and had collected enough, to go into business on his own. By the early seventies, his eye for the collectible object had become well known.

In the course of his business in Toronto, Wolf rarely bought or sold modern works at all. This did not prevent him from being on far too many mailing lists. He received notices announcing every sort of show, even student art displays. Normally he threw them away. One day, however, he was struck by the image on a card — a reproduction of a lithograph of finely drawn faces that were human, yet were not, for in an eerie way they were also the faces of birds. A talent out of the ordinary, he thought.

His heart sank when he walked into the College of Art for that opening. The room was crowded with Torontonians working up to an echo of the Haight-Ashbury effect, and as for the work — true to the ethos of the times, it let everything hang out except technique, he told himself. He would have turned and left right then, but he felt someone's eyes on him. A very tall young man was looking at him from across the room. Hollow-eyed — a face that strangely echoed the drawing on the invitation — a man of maybe twenty-five, with reasonable hair for those times. Then the young man pushed through all those people, took Wolf by the arm. "No, please," he said, "just let me show you before you go." He led Wolf to an alcove where five of the bird lithographs hung.

And what hit Wolf most forcefully, at that moment, was something it would seem he had always known, but oh so uselessly: the terrific erotic power a piece of art can have, a power not connected to the content, not at all, but released by every taut, surprising line.

As Wolf comes slowly awake in his room at Punta Verde, he is aware that this moment from the past has been given back to him in his dream. Or rather, he was dreaming that he was in his kitchen in Toronto. There was something very significant about the black-and-white tiles. But the feeling of that dream

— the feeling that clings round him even now — is the same dark, rich, optimistic sense of...well, there is hardly any word for it but *magic*, he has to say, though he blenches at the word. The sense that the world is about to open, that everything will change, for no reason you understand. Completely unplanned, undeserved. That powerful feeling a dream can lay upon you, which seems so much more important than what is actually there.

Wolf lies in bed and looks up at the fan, and then over at the wedges of sky shifting and re-forming behind some banana leaves outside. All of this he sees through a scrim of black and white. Those tiles. And he feels unaccountably happy. He has no idea what this means.

Breakfast is laid out on a long table on the covered terrace. Platters of pineapple, melon, papaya, all glistening. Pitchers of juice, freshly squeezed. A ceramic pot keeping warm the *gallo pinto*, the traditional mixture of rice and small black beans. Nelson is standing by to bring anything else you might like — a boiled egg, maybe, to go on top of the rice and beans. And coffee, freshly roasted Costa Rican coffee, which may well be the best in the world.

And everything gleams. Everything looks absolutely newly washed, each leaf of the thousand different kinds of leaf growing on the slope below looks washed and waxed and polished. *What can be the matter with me?* Wolf asks. Everything looks wonderful and smells delicious, as if he's been slipped a Prozac in his sleep. A great weight has been lifted, and he can hardly remember what that was. *Yes, you were absolutely right,* he says. *That attack of conscience was getting to be a frigging bore.*

There are some new arrivals this morning, or at least guests who were not at dinner. A party of Canadians comes in — they are obviously Canadians — who must be part of a nature tour. They have kind, earnest faces, and their voices carry, though in fact they are not too loud. They wear canvas hats, and blue jeans or stretchy tannish walking pants, pockets bulging with guidebooks, maps and Swiss Army knives. Yesterday they were in the cloud forest. They are quizzing one another on the plants they have seen. Regarding birds, they have seen everything they hoped for except a quetzal. The closest they came was to sight a team from *National Geographic* perhaps a hundred feet above the ground, in a tall vine-laden tree where they had been nesting for some days in the hope of photographing that rare bird.

There is a man sitting by himself who catches Wolf's eye. Wolf thinks there is something familiar about this figure — a thin dark man, not old, not young, with a face that strikes him as German, possibly. A face that is lean but does not look ascetic. This man is wearing an expensive panama hat, a silk shirt in a blue-and-green Tahitian print, deep blue trousers that look like lightweight wool. He is reading Thursday's *Miami Herald*.

Well, when you are on holiday you look at people, don't you? Wolf thinks. There's not much else to do.

The Danish banker and the lovely woman with the cap of golden hair are buttering thin sticks of some sort of packaged health bread (did they bring that with them from Denmark?) without exchanging a word. How rapidly the sweetness soured. He is reading a week-old *Herald Tribune*; she is studying a knitting magazine.

That group of khaki-clad men Wolf took for foreign correspondents yesterday are associated with some aid group. Food seems to be their speciality. They are discussing the price of lobster in Managua. That is how you tell the state of the economy there, they say. There is no sign of either Maddy or Irene. Yet as Wolf studies those men, Irene's voice comes barging in. *Walterson was there. He said he didn't know where you had got to.* Walterson, who was said to file his Sandinista profiles out of the bar of the Intercontinental — just the one to hit the pathos button about the situation in Toronto, but get the facts all wrong.

As Wolf thinks of Walterson, he pushes his *gallo pinto* away.

He must have been impressed, though. Walterson. You could hardly help but be impressed by that primrose room where death was held off by every device, terrestrial and extra-, it was possible to buy. For André has chosen to end his days with the scion of a grocery empire who is doing nicely marketing the essences of crystals.

To give Walterson his due, Wolf did not get the whole true picture himself, not for a long time. He hung around and hung around. He still wanted to be liked. He tried to see things from every side. Indeed there was much in what they said. Hadn't he always known that André — with a talent so exacting there was hardly any circumstance where it could flower; with his restless nature; with that need to feed not just something physical but his entire creative entity — that André was a creature one could lose but not contain? *This is my death, Wolfman*, André told him. *It's the last thing I'm going to do.*

"This is his death, Wolf," echoed the king of New Age marketing. "He does not need the confused vibrations he is getting from you now."

"Mr. Lazarus? Mr. Charles Lazarus?" Nelson is crossing the terrace, displaying an envelope, looking questioningly around. As if he didn't know exactly who this Charles Lazarus was supposed to be. Yet Wolf himself feels confused, as if he has brought someone into being who is now setting off on independent doings. For who on earth knows him by that name, or even knows he is here? As Nelson makes his way among the tables, the thin dark man in the linen jacket looks up expectantly. Wolf has a terrific urge to duck, turn away. He gulps the rest of his coffee, gets up to leave.

"Ah, Mr. Lazarus! There you are, man." Nelson lays the envelope beside his crumpled napkin. Wolf sees that it is one of the hotel's own envelopes.

Inside, in Maddy's looping backhand, he reads, *I'll be a little late, dear. Can we make it around two? That will give you time to go down to the sea this morning if you want. Thank you SO much* — underlined three times — *Love, M.*

She will be a little late. Only that. Well, why doesn't she just come outside and tell him? In the bright light of day this strikes Wolf as overboard and unnecessarily hard on his nerves, this cloak-and-dagger stuff.

No I will not go down to the sea, Wolf decides. Receiving that note has stirred up his old anxieties and added some new ones, which he tries to relieve by spinning a fantasy. Something is happening at the hotel that he has to keep an eye on. There may be more messages for this fictitious person, this Charles Lazarus, and then Wolf would have to be there to receive them; or perhaps "intercept" would be a better word. He elaborates on this, to take his mind from other things — but there is a jangling edge of true neurosis to it, too. He is a cautious man by nature, but so many times his life has spun out of control.

When he gets back to his room, he changes into a small red bathing suit, hardly more than a strip. He will spend the day by the pool. He goes close to the mirror, examines every part of his body, back and front. Then he begins the series of exercises he performs every day: bends his knees, touches his toes, puts himself through various yoga positions, culminating in the Lion.

As he lies on his back with his head poking out between his heels, holding the position of the Plough, he thinks of the fat woman, the one André would like to see him locked up in a train with. She and her husband came in to breakfast while Wolf was halfway through his meal, and they surely loaded up their plates. A pile of fruit, then back for beans — then calling merrily for eggs, croissants, pots of jam.

It is easy to mock that kind of hunger, and he did, and no doubt he will again. But as he flips his body up into the shoulder stand, then settles into the lotus position for the spell of meditation he imposes on himself almost every day — a period when the mind must be held completely blank, when any thought, if it comes into the head, must be observed like a passing cloud (*Oh well there it is,* you're supposed to say, before you look away) — he is again a ten-year-old back in Berlin. This is after the years of bombing; after the dull roar from the east, closer and closer every day, had become the reality of Russian soldiers pounding on the door, demanding watches in the first wave, and in the next searching out the women and girls. This is after his mother had decided it was safe to order his sisters out of hiding, to go into the country-side and scrounge for food. They are back, Rosel and Lisi. They come into the kitchen without a word. Lisi's dress, a pretty dirndl, has been torn right off her at the front. She is just thirteen years old. "Rosel ran and got away, but they gave me some bread," she says.

Flesh. There is no escape from it. Even as he's trying to escape it, he is obsessively keeping up the tone of it. This strikes Wolf as absurd. He uncoils, stands up, rubs his hip joint, which was threatening to lock. He has never figured out the conundrum, the way attention to the body can both save you and wreck you — oh, and please do not talk to him about discipline. Discipline is like a bomb, discipline is like the atom waiting to explode.

When Mutti died, Wolf did every single thing a free person might do. This is another thing he does not want to think about, now or any time.

Of course there had been encounters previously. Tantalizing moments of what looked like recognition. Brief conjunctions. Disappointing, all of them. He knew there were avenues of enchantment and surprise that he had not had the nerve or chance to explore till then. He did not think that meant just fucking. The chance meeting, maybe even in the dark, opening the door to something mystical if brief. The stranger. The touch that would know you. The touch that fathomed you completely, though you need not even see his face. That fantasy had lived with him for years.

Wolf took a trip after his mother died. He thought he would live one life in Toronto and another elsewhere. He left the business in the charge of his new assistant, a charming Irishwoman with a moustache, who had completed an apprenticeship at Christie's and was thrilled at this shot at responsibility. (An outsider, just like Wolf. Over the years they came to work together splendidly.) The mecca was San Francisco then, in that time before the plague. Wolf stayed at the

Clift and made forays down to Market, but the scene in the
Castro area alarmed him at first. I do not fit in anywhere, he
thought, not even here. Maybe especially not here. He per-
ceived something clubby, almost hearty, about the pumped-
up swaggering atmosphere.

He would have liked, at the opera or ballet, to have someone slide into the seat beside him. He drank, instead. Alcohol
had been a manageable, if increasing, habit up to then. Now
it gave him courage, propelled him into bars he never would
have dreamed of entering otherwise, made him handsome,
witty, liberal; made commerce seem attractive, not just essential; brought him the company of many strangers but never
the one he was looking for.

No, he does not want to remember how, soon, there was
no boundary between pleasure and self-destruction, how that
went on and on until at last he was a rag swollen up with
terror, nothing more.

When he finally pulled himself together, he did it all at
once. All those hearty virtues his mother had attempted to
embrace as the easy life slipped away, everything he had hoped
to escape — bodybuilding, exercise, abstinence, the grim en-
thusiastic business of saying yes to life as she dragged him
from Bad Gastein to Biarritz to Stresa — became the tools for
his rescue. He stayed in Toronto; he created himself anew. He
fabricated a creature somewhat old-fashioned and courtly,
good-mannered to a fault. And all of this was tempered, as
his needs settled down, by that hoard of detailed knowledge
he had accumulated as if this might be the saving grace of
life. If he preserved an empty space inside, he told himself
that also kept him afloat.

You have been dead, you delightful Wolfman....

Had there been the remotest chance that he would turn
away, when an opportunity to blow apart his safe dead life
presented itself to him?

Wolf lies by the pool and bakes first one side then the other,
just like the Danes, only not bothering with creams. His tor-
por is an active thing. He feels the breeze change direction.

Banana leaves rustle. The sun bakes through his bones. He watches an iguana as it moves along the wall of the terrace where the pool is cantilevered out above the jungle. The lizard moves, then pauses. Its head bobs up and down. The delicate brown fingers spread on the stone and then at length the muscles tauten, the iguana takes a step, its head bobs up and down again. Wolf understands that this is fast, perhaps excessive progress. What is vital is to be sandwiched between the hot stone and the sun.

If you like it here, señor....

My name is Wolf. I would like you to call me Wolf, por favor.

If you like it here, we can come back tomorrow, Señor *Wolf. They owe me some time from the hotel, and my cousin likes to rent the boat.*

Then I will pay you, Manuel. I will pay you for your time, and I will pay your cousin for the boat.

Señor *is very kind.*

Sometimes Wolf attempts to read. He has found the book the boy took along when they went to the islands. That was a lovely thing, the way they read in turns, the boy correcting Wolf's pronunciation and translating, with beautiful fresh images, stories of life in the far hills and valleys of this country, stories children read in school, yet there was a sense of horror Wolf could not quite grasp, a sense of menace, of remote people face to face with God. Belief is so very strong in this country, strong and practical. "I do wish I could stay here forever," Wolf had said idly to the boy. "Oh, well then you must make a bargain with God," the boy had replied. "That is what I do. When I wanted to get the job at the hotel, I promised that I would give half of my first week of pay to the poor." "And did you do that?" "I would have, but my father took it first. But I am keeping count. I will pay everything I owe."

It is just an exercise, now, for Wolf to force his mind along the sentences of those simple but baffling children's tales — a form of discipline that has the quick reward of putting him to sleep, though not for long.

It is quiet at the poolside. Most of the guests from last night have either checked out or headed to the beaches, but that can't be where the large religious writer has taken himself off to. He would never make it down the trail. He will be rapping out uplifting chapters in his room, Wolf supposes. But the wife — who has covered herself in acres of jungle print since breakfast — was at the pool when Wolf arrived, and for quite a while he has been willing her to leave. Look at her, in another garment big enough to wrap a bridge. She seems to be some sort of artist. She is sketching the iguana. She works fast; this does not have the air of a hobby. She is one of those who has to record things in order to make them real. She will not have been here, not at all, until she gets this safely recorded in her sketchbook — and even then, Wolf thinks, can she claim to have experienced a thing?

This makes him feel better and infinitely worse. Holy Jesus, smug little bastard. He sees the island off Coco, the rolling glassy stretch of sea — the rocks, the hidden beach — the way the sun turned black and still poured down. He hears someone, a drowned man, shouting for joy.

He believes he has not let the iguana out of his sight, yet it is gone. The fat woman has turned her gaze on Wolf. He shifts out of the way, behind a line of chairs.

He is not hungry for lunch today. *Perhaps I should begin a fast,* he thinks. He cannot believe he is thinking this. Exactly as it came over Mutti, is it now coming over him once more? Can we escape nothing in this world? Does it all go round and round and round? One day his mother was drinking champagne with a gentleman from New York who had helped her onto the streetcar in Munich, *a very cultured person,* she told Wolf, *a publisher!* The next, or so it seemed, she was informing the manager of Bernheimer's that Wolf would have to take a leave of absence, for she needed him to accompany her on a medical cure. She did this without discussing it with Wolf. When Wolf was called up to the office, it was all arranged. "We will welcome you back," Herr Dietzmann said, "but obviously your dear mother cannot be expected to undertake this trip alone." Wiesbaden quickly proved too expensive. Next stop, Montecatini Terme. In a park once frequented by the Medici, in a neo-Greek temple dedicated to rejuvenation, he watched his mother drink sulphur water from a calibrated spa glass, then rush to one of the *gabinetti* for the purge, then return to drink another. Wolf had a secret by then. He had met a gentleman himself, who had given him a silver flask. *Just to ensure against an overdose of well-being, my dear young friend.*

It is two-fifteen and Maddy still has not arrived; there has been no sign of her all day. If she went out to the market, she should have been before this. But then, if she was going out to the market, why didn't she ask Wolf to go? Quite often he went along to help her, when he was here in other years. And on these outings Maddy came alive: bargained in her execrable Spanish, flashed her eyes. *Guapa, guapa...!* Wolf remembers the egg man whispering as he watched her walk away; and she herself must have been aware of indrawn breaths as she made her way through the crowd. On the way home they would stop at a roadside cantina. What did they talk about? She never talked about her past. How peculiar, Wolf thinks now; I told her many things about my life when I was young, but I did not learn a single item about her. How self-engrossed I have always been. Yet the impression he'd had back then was that they made a perfect team. They did not talk about the present. Maddy did not talk about Irene. Wolf did not talk about André. It was as if they were conspiring, without a word or gesture, to stretch a seal tighter than Saran Wrap over any personal thing. Oh those jewel-like early mornings, André still grumpy, feigning sleep.

Wolf has just decided that he is miffed when suddenly there she is, at the far end of the pool. She is wearing a large one-piece bathing suit, black. She is standing tucking her hair into a bulging old-fashioned rubber cap with a strap at the chin. She waves to him, and dives in. Her skin is that grey that skin turns in the tropics when it never gets the sun. In the water, though, she looks sleek as a seal.

She does twenty laps of the pool at least, without ever looking his way. This is how beauties behave, he knows that, though she has never been this way with him. Ex-beauties, anyway. Or maybe ex-beauties particularly. Keeping people waiting, to prove things they never needed to prove before. When she finally clambers out she wraps herself quickly, shakes out her hair, puts on a dashing high-crowned hat in the Nicaraguan style. A waiter brings a white metal chair.

"So how are you doing?" Her smile turns up all the oddness of life, just like that, in a ripple. A quick smile that quickly closes down again, but he forgives her right away.

She is not wearing dark glasses. Her eyes seem to him to have developed a protective misty film. "Soda?" she says brightly, as if this were a play.

"Now Maddy, this will not do," he says.

"I know," she says. "I'm just putting off the moment. Once I say it, it's done." No mention of his own sadness, bereavement, guilt. Thank goodness.

"You had better say it, then."

For this is just what he needs. Action. Somebody taking action, and certainly not him. *We have all merely drifted along the way that life has swept us*, is the feeling percolating below his conscious thoughts, *and it is time that someone put a stop to that.*

"Well, if you *could* lend me some money...," she says.

"How much do you need?"

"I need a lot, actually. I'm leaving for good, you see."

"Where are you going, though?"

"Well, I've packed my stuff, such as it is — and in about five minutes I'm going to swipe her Jeep and head up the back road to San José."

"You don't need to say 'swipe'. It must be as much yours as hers."

"No no no, Wolf. Everything is hers."

"Maddy, that is not the way it works any more. You have worked here as an equal partner, for what? Years and years? Half this *place* should be yours."

"Not to hear her talk. She put all the money in. I'm just the pretty face." She laughs and runs her hand across her eyes, and shakes her head.

"But has she threatened you? Is that it? Are you afraid for

your safety?"

"Oh no, Wolf. Nothing like that. Nothing physical. Unless you count this...." She makes a gesture that includes the whole of her, her face, her thickened body. "But I'm nothing. I'm no one. Can you imagine how it feels to be no one."

Wolf doesn't know what to say to this. *Why now?* he wonders. Why all of a sudden has being no one become so terrible? Various possibilities occur, but he does not want to cause pain by asking her. What is the attraction over at the house of the lawyer in Quetal? Someone the spitting image of Maddy twenty years ago? Isn't that the way it works? If so, you could say that Maddy is the victim, but at the same time didn't she take the easy way? Didn't she work here like a drudge, on and on — perhaps never say a thing? Wolf is an expert on the easy way. You say nothing. You say it again and again and again.

She reaches out, takes his hand. Her nails are perfect despite all the work he thinks she has done, the softest shade of pearl. "Don't look so worried," she says. "I'm being overdramatic. I'll be okay."

"Look, Maddy — of course, I will do anything you want. I can let you have five hundred cash. And then...let me see. If you could wait until the weekend is over, I could go to a bank for you...."

"No! Now that I've made my mind up, I've got to get out of this jeezly place today!"

"Then let me come along with you...."

"No darling, really. I don't want that. I only get to do this once. I've got to do it on my own." *It's my death, Wolfman...*is the echo he hears; he has no place in anyone's drama. Then he wants to kick himself.

"What will you do in San José?"

"I'm going home to Canada. I'm getting the bloody hell out of here." And her face as she says this is so determined that she looks pretty once again. And Wolf thinks, *Yes, yes she can do it. This is wonderful. One should never lose faith in people's ability to change.*

"Well then, I believe travellers' cheques are the best thing I can do. Suppose I endorse...two thousand dollars over to you? That should get you on the plane and take care of a hotel for a night or two. Go to the embassy, if the bank gives you trouble. I will give you my business card; and I will write a note as well, shall I?" But then he wishes he had not said that. He will have to renege — not on the money, but on the note, even the card. It might not be all that smart to shout his present whereabouts. Well, maybe she will forget that part of it. "Ah, and I've got it!" he adds quickly. "When you get to Toronto you can stay at my house for a while. That would be splendid. I hate leaving it empty, anyway. Will you do that? Maddy, it turns out you are an answer to prayer."

"You dope!" she says. "An answer to prayer! What a con man. God, why didn't you and I just team up years ago?"

"Ah Maddy. What a thought!"

"But look, Wolf — of course this is only a loan, you know. Once I get on my feet up there, I'll pay you back in...what do you suggest, pirogis? If nothing better comes along."

"I believe I would prefer those little pastry swans."

"You've got it. Swans. But now I'd better get inside. You know, it's murder what the sun does to my skin."

An hour later, Wolf is feeling considerably shaken — too shaken to take the steep path down to the beach this afternoon, though on the other hand he does not want to be around when Irene returns.

Helping Maddy did seem to be a brave and good idea when he was caught up in it, when he was making out the cheques. But then she kept dawdling. He tried to hurry her along. He collected her bags from the apartment where she and Irene lived. He had never been in there before. She led him around the back, along a gravel path that skirted the hill. The path was edged with tall red lilies. "We planted those when we first came here," she said. There was a stone patio back there, and slatted wooden doors led into a sitting room with chintz-covered furniture, quite pleasant. He could see a large bedroom beyond, a wide white bed, sheer curtains drawn open to give a splendid view out over the sea. Maddy led him into a dark bedroom in behind, with a single window that looked back towards the slope. Her bags were sad — a set of old-fashioned matching Samsonite hard-sided cases in pearly tan, each case smaller than the next, three of them, and a round hat-box, and a square top-handled makeup case as well. The cases had hardly been used. They looked like the sort of thing she might have received as a graduation gift from high school — and their big adventure was a scandalous exit to Costa Rica, and now they were going home.

When all her things were stowed, Maddy left him by the car and went back inside the hotel lobby one more time. "No, I'll be a sec," she said. "There's nothing more to carry. Just a quick trip to the ladies'." Wolf waited, with a skulking sensation, a little way down the path. She looked nervous as she came out. She glanced behind her, fiddling with the large leather shoulder-bag she was carrying; he hadn't noticed that before. She wedged the bag into the back with some care, among all the others but behind her seat. Then she turned and embraced him, and he helped her up into the car. She was wearing a denim dress, and a Tilley hat that some guest had left behind. "Don't worry — if I fall into the water I'll float" was the last thing he heard her say, before she drove away.

Wolf is not sure why he went through the lobby on his way back to the pool. He was wearing his bathing suit. It would have made sense to go around the outside way.

The lobby was deserted. At that hour of the afternoon, Corazón, the desk clerk, was having her siesta, and if you wanted help with anything you were supposed to ring the bell.

The lobby was empty, and so was the case where the jade gods had lived all these years. The light inside the case was on, shining on the black stone surface that held nothing at all. And Wolf was trying to think. Had he suspected something when he'd walked in here? Was that why he'd come this way? When had he last looked at this case, anyway? Had he come in here this morning?

Empty. He couldn't believe it. Was there something he should do? Ring the bell, let someone know?

But come on, he is telling himself now. Surely this is a

tempest in an inkpot, or whatever the damned expression is. If Maddy took the jade, so what? *If it was worth taking, though, that must mean it was genuine after all.*

But no matter — didn't she deserve whatever she could get? Hadn't he told her more or less that, a little while ago? Why should he be thinking that she had fooled him in some way, by taking money from him as well? Of course she would need the money, till she got all the rest worked out. And very honourably, very thoughtfully, she did not want to implicate him in her scheme.

Except wasn't he implicated by helping her get away?

Nelson is approaching, and Wolf has to resist the urge to pretend to be asleep, even though the boy has already caught his eye.

"Is there anything you'd like?" is all Nelson says. "Fruit juice, soda, lemonade?"

"Ah, more soda, thank you — *pero, sin hielo,* if you please; absolutely without ice, *por favor.*"

Yes, as Wolf drinks down a whole bottle of soda he realizes that he was shaking, but maybe it was dehydration, plain thirst. He should move out of the sun, but at the same time, right now, he needs the way it is slamming him.

There was almost continuous bombing for the last three years of the war. That is the way Wolf remembers it, at least. The house where he lived was on a hill, outside of town. The centre of the city was the target, and the industrial area, of course. Still, Wolf and his sisters and his mother lived with a constant sense of danger; everyone did.

"Could you see the bombing going on?" Maddy asked him once. "From where you lived?" Maybe she thought you watched it the way people watch fireworks now.

"Well you know, you are not very interested," Wolf said, "when you have to get up three times a night to go to the shelter."

The house directly behind had the neighbourhood siren. The sound of that still goes through Wolf's head; any foolish thing can set it off, some irrational worry or fear. You had to get up, half asleep — get dressed in the cold and damp — always thinking that this time, when it was over, the house might be gone. But even if you went to the shelter, there was a chance that you too might be gone.

Behind the house was the *wasch-küche,* where the weekly wash was done — or cooked, literally. The hut housed a huge copper kettle under which a fire was lit, so the laundry could be boiled. That building — reinforced with concrete for the purpose (a job that Uncle Hansel had overseen) — was where they went night after night when the siren sounded. They all had cots in there, Wolf and his mother and the girls. Sometimes, though, if Uncle Hansel was in the house when the siren sounded, he would carry Wolf out, still in his pyjamas, and put the boy straight into his cot. Wolf was a small boy for his age, and he was only nine years old then — on the night he is thinking of right now.

There was just one dim light in the *wasch-küche,* hanging from the ceiling in the centre of the room. Wolf's cot was in the shadows, on the far side of the great copper pot. In the distance he could hear the explosions, on and on, *but on the other side of the river, little* Dummkopf — *they will never want to drop them here,* his mother said. Wolf could feel the explosions as well as hear them. He could feel the floor of the wash house tremble; he could see the way the lightbulb stopped in the middle of its swaying when a bomb hit the ground, as if the light was jerked to attention. He imagined he could see the bulb literally jump on its cord before it began its hypnotic swaying once again.

If Wolf worked everything correctly in his mind, though, he could make the wash house turn into a cosy cave. He was a cave boy, safe in the shadows. His sisters fretted, argued, in their cots over by the cupboard where the folded sheets and towels were kept. To pass the time and keep their spirits up they sang silly songs. His mother smoked cigarette after cigarette, until the air was blue, and flipped the pages of five-year-old fashion magazines. But the cave boy, in his shadowy place, reached his hands inside his pyjamas and began the secret process that would make all of that go away.

He knew he should not do it. Already, horribly, his mother

had taken him to task. This had been much earlier, when he was a very little child. The picture in his mind of that shameful event had him sitting in his own chair by the tile stove in the drawing room, looking at a picture book about a family of bears and how they all cuddled up for the winter. Wolf was wearing a fine suspendered pair of lederhosen that Uncle Hansel had brought for him from Austria. His mother and Uncle Hansel were talking in those hissing voices he loathed. They were having another fight. That meant that in a moment she would start to weep, and then they would leave the room and go upstairs, and Wolf would be left alone.

Wolfschen — what are you doing? Suddenly they were both looking straight at him. He dropped the book into his lap. He whipped away his hand. *Were you fondling yourself? Hans, was he* fondling *himself? What am I going to do? Trying to be mother and father to this boy, and now he is playing with himself. And my only friend — the only person I believed I could trust in this bitter world — has hired a Brunnhilde for his office and finds the pressure of work has become extreme...!* And then she did begin to weep, and Uncle Hansel led her away. But not before he had paused and leaned over Wolf's chair. He took both Wolf's hands in his. He examined them and dropped them. He gave Wolf's face a slap.

To make it work, the cave boy had to pretend that he was not in a narrow iron cot; he had to be in a big soft bed of leaves or furs, with someone large — his father? He could hardly remember his father, but he thought he could recall his father's smell: a dark tobacco smell, an impression of sadness and rumpledness. So in his cave bed he was cuddled by his father sometimes, and that would cheer his father up. Or else he'd be held by some other large and furry creature that loved him and kept him safe, perhaps a bear.

The air raid was over. The siren sounded the all-clear. It was very late, maybe two or three. Mutti was rousing the girls. "Can't we stay?" they said. "Can't we sleep out here for once, oh please?" "Oh for pity's sake," Mutti said, "do you expect me to spend the whole night here in this chair?" The girls were protesting, but struggling into their winter boots and coats. Wolf pretended to be asleep. *Perhaps they will forget me,* he thought. He wouldn't mind; he wanted to stay there in his cave and be forgotten. He *was* half asleep, probably. Uncle Hansel was there that night. Wolf had pretended to be asleep when Uncle Hansel carried him out here, earlier, and Uncle Hansel had wrapped Wolf's limp arms around his neck, though Wolf kept letting them slip down. Uncle Hansel had carried Wolf on his hip, using his left hand to close the door behind him, clasping Wolf tight against his body by the pressure of his arm, the long bony fingers of his other hand tightly cupping Wolf's bum.

"Wolfschen, Wolfschen," his mother started calling.

"Oh why not leave the boy?" Uncle Hansel said. "You know he already has a cold. Why should we drag him out of bed again? I'll stay here, Leni. Look — I still have work to do anyway." He had brought his briefcase with him on his visit, and after the raid started he had worked at the wooden table that was there for folding up the wash, while he waited for the all-clear.

"I never see you," Wolf's mother whispered harshly. "You promise that you'll come, and then you spend the night out here."

His glasses glittered. "Please do not harass me any further, Leni. I have work to do, and I have already had too many interruptions. Now go on into the house, and leave me, please."

His mother left.

Uncle Hansel lit a cigarette, pulled out his chair, sat at the table. Wolf drifted off to sleep again, his body curled up like a shrimp beneath the covers, his two hands between his legs where the little creature, as he called it — for it had a life all its own — had spent itself an hour earlier, at the height of the raid. He woke to find the blanket pulled away, Uncle Hansel glaring down.

"So. Just as I thought." As if to someone else in the room. "Leni's boy plays with himself, still. I would not be at all surprised if the boy grew up to be a queer."

He grabbed Wolf by the arm and pulled him out of bed. "Is that the situation, Wolfschen?" he said. "Do you look at other little boys?"

"I...don't know what you mean." But Wolf believed perhaps he did, though at the same time he didn't have the least idea what was going on. He didn't look at little boys, he looked at big boys. He got a lovely but despairing feeling when he looked at the leader of his youth group, when that dark-haired fellow with his beautiful pale face and deep blue eyes got them marching, shouted at them to straighten their backs. Was this bad? He had suspected it was wrong.

"I think you do know what I mean. The apple of his mother's eye — but look what a rotten little thing he is. Well, I believe it's time he learned a thing or two." He had swung Wolf up so he was standing on the bed with his face close to his own. His breath was odd and gassy. Wolf was thinking of the moon — not the real one, but the one he sometimes drew, with a thin curved face that was funny when Wolf drew it; he usually gave it a beaky nose, a round and smiling eye, an eyebrow raised in happy surprise. Uncle Hansel's face was not like that, but Wolf was telling himself that he could erase it, change it, when he realized that he had wet his pants. And Uncle Hansel was unbuckling his leather belt. Wolf was going to get a thrashing.

But Wolf didn't get a thrashing. With a couple of swift decisive moves, Uncle Hansel stripped off Wolf's soaking wet pyjamas and swung him around and bent him over the table and held him down and rammed his creature up the hole of Wolf's bum. Wolf knew it was his creature, that hot hard tearing thing, because he had caught a glimpse of it when Uncle Hansel dropped his trousers: a long inflamed neck, a stubby flaring head. He'd seen his uncle spit on his hand and wet it before he rammed it in.

This was something that Wolf had never dreamed, though he'd had other wicked thoughts. It hurt worse than anything Wolf had ever imagined. This was the punishment for thinking all those things. "This is what it's like, if you intend to get into that," his Uncle Hansel said. "If you think you'd like to be a bum-boy, I'd better show you how it is."

The pain went on and on. "Ach, you make me sick," his uncle said when he was finished. "Go back to bed and go to sleep. If you don't stop crying, I will call your mother and tell her that her beloved son is a little pervert."

Yet afterwards, though he was sick and confused — though he pleaded with his mother not to make him go to school, so that for a week she kept him home and babied him, believing that his fever (yes, he really had a fever) was the flu — he could not stop thinking of how strong his uncle was; how he had clicked his heels and made his mother leave and lied to her; how he had held Wolf by the shoulders, how he had breathed in his ear and told Wolf he was a filthy filthy little boy, before he stuck his tongue in there; how he had shuddered, how Wolf had seen tears running down his uncle's cheeks before he turned on Wolf in anger once again and ordered him back to bed. And a week later, when his uncle came for dinner (food was becoming scarce by then — already refugees from the eastern provinces, with all their belongings piled onto wagons or into baby-carriages, had begun their desperate flight, and thousands of them, starving, dying, trailed through the outskirts of Berlin day after day — but Uncle Hansel always arrived with a hamper of delicious things), Wolf could tell from the way his uncle kept looking at him that Uncle Hansel could not help thinking about what had happened either.

When dinner was over, "I think I will take Wolf with me when I drive to the country tomorrow," Uncle Hansel said. "Von Heimach is ill, and I have to visit him. He has some papers there for me." The next day was Sunday. Wolf would not have to go to school.

The expression on Mutti's face. Von Schlichting had paid very little attention to her Wolfschen up to then, except to regard him as an overly watchful presence, frequently in the way — not like the daughters, who had friends and activities, but a bookish loner, always around the house.

"He has been home from school all week," she protested. She did not like things she didn't understand. "Besides, if you are going to the country, why don't we all come along?" But she said this tentatively. All evening she had sensed something different in his manner, and she could not get along without Von Schlichting now — how would they eat? And he had promised to take care of them, and get them out of there, if the Russians were truly advancing in the way the forbidden short-wave broadcasts said.

"Leni, the boy is getting soft. You said so yourself. He needs to get out a bit. He needs a man's company. I will take him to the country and see he gets some good fresh air."

"Wolfschen? What do you say? Do you want to go to the country with Uncle Hansel tomorrow?" She burst out laughing, over-bright. "Maybe he will let you wear his hat."

Wolf kept looking at his knife. He didn't say yes or no. When he glanced over finally, his uncle was looking at him with a new expression. Maybe what had happened had been a mistake. Or maybe Wolf *had* been bad, and now the punishment was over and Uncle Hansel would teach him to be good. He was scared. He remembered how his uncle's breath had smelled. But then he thought of how it had felt when Uncle Hansel had held him, just for a moment, at the end. He got down from his chair, without saying "Excuse me" or anything, and went over and climbed into his uncle's lap. "Oh, will you look at that!" his mother said.

Maybe it wasn't Maddy who took away the jade. Maybe Irene took the effigies to show whoever she is meeting today. Maybe she decided to sell them, all perfectly above-board. Wolf can imagine how she would work that — always holding to the belief that they were reproductions, yet not at all interested in letting them go except for an outrageous price. Was it her fault if they were smuggled out of the country after that?

She had a variety of stories of how she had acquired the pieces, always vague. "Oh, we came across them when we were excavating for the pool...." Wolf met a woman in Toronto to whom Irene had told that. And in some ways that was likelier than the story of the sleazy German in the hotel lobby. *My God*, he thinks, *but I have been blind.* All these years, because he wanted her to like him, he has failed to give the matter the critical attention it deserved. There had been that settlement, exactly here. What if Irene had found herself in possession of a remarkable archaeological site? That bib of gold she used to wear, which she had also passed off vaguely

if anyone mentioned how authentic it looked. *Oh come on —
who do you think I am?* What if she had rifled a hoard of treasures, and then calmly built her hotel on top? Wolf would like
to think that of her, now. It is a great help to think there
might be people worse than he is on every side.

Yes, and the fact is, she has never liked him, has she?
That remark years ago, about the way the bad Germans were
attracted here like flies, was no slip of the tongue. He worried
her, he thinks now. He was an expert on all the things she
wanted to keep vague.

The axe-gods are gone. Wolf thinks that has a fine apoca-
lyptic ring. At Punta Verde the gods have left already, and the
jungle is waiting to close in. He has this much of his mother
in him — he is thinking of Mutti's susceptibility to omens,
now — that when he walked in the first time and saw the
jade, he experienced one of those odd flashes that tell you,
Yes, you are here. Of course, the feeling comes and goes. All
you are left with is the memory of the feeling, not the flash
of insight that was surely there as well. You have no idea why
you felt for a moment that the most important event of your
life might happen here.

Now he is moving in and out of sleep. The faces of the
small jade gods become the faces André used to draw, the
beaks, the staring eyes. Yet they keep their knife-sharp surfaces. And no one knows what these were used for, Wolf is
thinking in his dream (he is walking a hall of mirrors), but all
at once he gets a flash, just as when he first walked into the
lobby and saw the small carved shapes. They are the thing
you can take hold of, if you are brave enough to grasp the
edge. In fact, they are the edge. They are the conundrum of
the edge. They are the way André grappled with the edge — *I
am touching the eternal in the present,* his voice is saying, though
André never said that. The mask splits open to show the in-
tent face with which he stalked his fate.

BUT I LOVED HIM.

Wolf sits up, glances warily around. Did he actually shout
that out? No one is looking his way.

There is so little movement by the pool that the iguana
has reappeared and crept forward to the very rim of turquoise

tile above the water. It bends its spiny head and peers down. It has a pattern like black lace thrown over its hump-backed surface, something Wolf failed to recognize before.

A day by the pool, in the most beautiful place in the world. Wolf leafs through the newspaper the man in the panama hat left on the table after breakfast. He comes upon a review of a revival of a Jules Feiffer play. "Why care about anyone else?" the review says is the message; "The only true feeling is no feeling. That is the only way to survive."

Wolf would like to keep an ear out for the return of Irene, but the music from the poolside speakers and the splashing of a group of *pensionados*, freshly arrived from San José but originally from the States, make that impossible. The new-comers have driven down the Puriscal Road — *if you can call that a road,* they exclaim. *Washouts, my God — you'd think the rainy season was yesterday. Nothing ever gets fixed in this country. You get crazy living here after a while,* they tell the newcomers in their midst, visitors from Kansas who are also thinking of moving down on the Costa Rican government's *pensionado* plan, which allows you to live pretty much tax-free. *And the way people drive. That Jeep that came at us on the wrong side, just above the banana plantations, Christ, burning up the road. Barney had to slam on the brakes so hard he nearly hit a cow.*

The afternoon spreads and spreads. Wolf is washed up in a vast surrealist landscape, bodies drooping over every horizontal surface, as more and more guests check in. And the seasons of Vivaldi seep from the speakers, then Pachelbel, then Boccherini, then spring, summer, autumn, winter once again, the world's greatest hits, on and on.

He has always been the waiting one. Waiting for the bombing to be over one more time; waiting for Von Schlichting to demand his company again, an axe of dread that hung over Wolf in the last months of the war. Did his mother guess what was going on? Do people ever see what they don't want to see? Waiting for his mother to die. Holding her hand and watching the berserk multiplying cells feed on the flesh of her lovely selfish face. Holding her hand, unable to stop seeing the gates of freedom swinging open, unable to bear her suffering, just wanting it to end *because I cannot stand this:* unable to keep those shameful words from running through his brain.

Waiting for the need to drink to die away, once he entered those years of sleepwalking calm before he met André. But it never truly died away. It has always been there, just beyond the rim of one more day.

Waiting for his mate to come home. Waiting for the phone to ring with the result of André's tests. (We'd like you to come in and see us, they said, and Wolf went along with him and waited that time too, sick with worry, confusion, anger, fear — *fear for your*self *you selfish little shit* — reading magazines on how to gold-leaf picture frames and candlesticks and boxes, how to get a complete new look by sewing ruffles onto anything that didn't move, how to make meatless casseroles.) Waiting around for months after that, even after André moved away, trying to decide what he would do.

His mate. That is what he said. How astounding that though he understood their bargain almost from the moment it was struck, and though he kept it, he always lived a kind of parallel existence of hope. And all his life he has been that way. The need for constancy, for true deep understanding focused just on him, is such a hardy little seed that nothing seems to kill it. What a disaster that is. The mosquito lays its eggs in swamps, and if the land dries up the eggs survive for decades, maybe even centuries, waiting for the right conditions to reappear. But the kind of hope that Wolf had — *Ach, well,* he says, *that could be worse than any of the other plagues.*

He climbed into that animal Von Schlichting's lap, and that was not enough to cure him. Von Schlichting was blown up in the Führer's bunker, or else he escaped to South America, God knows; but Wolf found himself in the same trap again and again.

Just last night, as he showered — as he looked at the frog clinging to the wall like a piece of interior decoration that was getting out of hand — he thought of his mother: of the fiction she had created for her life, of her ridiculous belief in omens as the years wore on. She would have made some-

thing of that frog. Wolf's story with André had aspects of the
classic fairy tale — the kingdom gained and, in return, the
transformation of the toad. But if Mutti had been telling it,
the impoverished artist who kissed a frog would at least have
gone on to fortune and acclaim.

But what more could Wolf have done?

André had been teaching a night class in printmaking
when they met. This was so that he himself could have ac-
cess to a press. He had arranged the show of prints so that his
own work could be seen. Wolf encouraged him to give up
teaching, built him a studio above the garage, bought him a
press, made sure he always had supplies, urged him to explore, to move from printmaking into oils. Wolf got him a
show with Harma Wilder, which almost any artist would kill
for, young or old. André would not let Wolf come up into his
studio during the time he was preparing. He withdrew from
the show a month before it was set to open. *I can not work
under that kind of commercial pressure,* he said. This drove Wolf
crazy. Oh, how sad it made him. André wasting his talents. It
became so personal; as if it were Wolf he was wasting in some
way — not the money, but much more.

For the truth was (Wolf is thinking now, perhaps for the
first time) that he fell in love with the work as much as with
the man. As his mouth travelled the body, he felt in touch
with the energy inside, as if all he had studied, traced and
worshipped, all his life, was in his bed now, pressed against
his skin. Something like that. Something you could kill, in
any case, by caring about it too much. *It's* my *art, Wolfman....*
That was the first echo of the final plea.

To have someone peer at you that way — the way Wolf
must have peered at André. To have the evanescent looked at
as if it were a crank that could be turned. No wonder André
would storm out into the night, be gone sometimes for days.
Rage. No wonder he turned on Wolf, driven wild, he said, by
what he called Wolf's prudery. Prudery not of action but of
language. *Say it,* he would yell, *say it say it say it, if you want it!
Admit out loud what you are.* This made Wolf stubborn, though
he knew better than to try to explain. Anyway, he did not
want to be put into any sort of defining box. He never went

with André on marches, demanding rights, expressing rage. And if André prowled as the years wore on (or always), Wolf did not want to know.

Wolf never had the nerve to make demands. He told himself that this was respect for human freedom: that none of us has the right to make others change. But the truth was that he could not stand it when André turned on him, or, worse, when he walked away. Wolf thought it was the finish, every time. He thought, at those times, not that André was wasting his talent, but that fear of his own talent was wasting André. He thought of the childhood his lover rarely talked about, such sadness there that it could kill a person, though Wolf never truly understood. The small village in New Brunswick, a village that was just one long straggle of shops and houses on either side of the highway, the church at the end. Particularly, André would never talk about the church. The meanest houses you could imagine, he said. When André went out into the night like that, Wolf would remember other nights, how for what seemed like hours he would hold his lover while he cried.

Then the switch, the change: André coming home with some outrageous present he had put on Wolf's Visa card. A stuffed iguana once. *Because I called and made reservations at Punta Verde*, he explained. *And they wired me this as confirmation. So we leave on Friday for two weeks. You know, you've been looking pretty peaked lately and, to tell you the truth, that gets me down.*

Wolf suffered. He suffered those intense anxieties and pains and worries that leave us in no doubt that we are real.

Maybe we never know what's going on in our lives from day to day. Maybe it takes years to get the true picture, and if we're lucky we never arrive at a situation where we have to. They went on and on, together. One would have to say "together," no matter what went on in truth. They went to the opera in their dinner jackets, they subscribed to the symphony, they had parties: Wolf did the cooking, André handed round the drinks. They took trips, whenever Wolf could get away. They had friends from all around the world who came and stayed.

But I loved him. That has almost the shock of a revelation. Wolf has spent so long bound up in jealousy and blame and fear.

At last the sky turns red. Everything falls still. Banana leaves and palm leaves and rattling bamboo wait, completely hushed, for the moment when the tropic coast swings into night.

The swimmers take their final swims, begin to drift away from the pool. The fat woman has occupied the same lounge chair almost all day long, busy with her sketchbook. Her method is to pick on those who do not know they are being watched. Wolf has been watching *her* — the way she turns her chair this way and that, the way she tenses, her whole enormous body straining forward eagerly, when some new person settles down within her range. She makes him think of an eager hunting dog. He would love to see what she has drawn; she has the air of someone going after faults and foibles. That pretty girl whose hip-bones jut out the fabric of her green bathing suit: has she been made into an anorexic? Has the focus been on the ducklike way she walks, and not on her splendid crinkled hair?

When the big woman stands at last, and has gathered up her gear and stowed it all into a Mexican bag, she pauses. She looks momentarily nonplussed, as if she wonders what is next, or what she is doing here. Then perhaps she remembers, *Oh yes of course, there's dinner.* She brightens. She heads off down the path with a look of purpose, and when she moves she is almost dainty. She is not wearing flat arch-supporting sandals; beneath her jungled acres her feet look tiny, in bright purple high-heeled shoes that flit along like butterflies.

What will happen about dinner, with Maddy gone? The thought of all the complications — let alone of facing Irene, who must be back by now — makes Wolf feel sick. One look at him, and she will know that he is in some way responsible. He is not in the least hungry, anyway. Perhaps he really has begun a fast today. A resolution made by default, while he was looking the other way.

He goes to the bar. He will collect some bottled water for

his room. He is parched again. Nervous and thirsty and ill at ease.

The boys behind the bar wear shorts and T-shirts. Their legs and arms and faces are varying dark shades. Nelson comes through from the kitchen carrying a crate of bottles. His arms bulge with exertion, yet he lifts this heavy burden with an easy swing. The play of his muscles is so beautiful. The tautness and whiteness of the clothing over this lithe well-muscled form — beautiful, beautiful.

All the boys turn and watch Wolf as he gives his order.

"Hey, hey," Nelson says, "you don't need to carry such a load. I can bring it to your room, enough bottles to last while you are here. I get my break in half an hour. I'll come then?"

The boys await the answer. There is not, on any face, the flicker of a change. And it could mean anything. And that is not the point. Signalling this, the sun falls beneath the water. The ocean stands up flat for a moment, backlit, a luminous blue-grey. How exhausting, the way any human resolve can over-turn, just like that.

"Ah thank you Nelson," Wolf hears himself say. "I will take merely what I can carry. And I would be grateful if you would cancel my place at dinner, if you please. I seem to have overdone the sun today."

How exhausting and terrible and pointless to have to go on and on and on, carrying this skinful of out-of-control wants and frailty.

⊶⊷ ⊶⊷

SUNDAY

Wolf's mother is wearing a black cocktail suit, a hat with a pin like the horn of a small unicorn. She walks into the dining room of El Más Hermoso with the perfect, totally misplaced demeanour that has always held him. Her back is very straight. Her nostrils flare. She comes and sits across from him at one of the pink wooden tables. He thinks how pale she looks. She should not be out like this. She puts a parcel on the table, a hexagonal box. Wolf realizes that the box contains something he has long been looking for, an Edo tea bowl. He reaches for the box. She snatches it away. He is appalled at how she handles it, although he knows the bowl will be wrapped in many layers of silk. She walks off, the box balanced on her head. *Not now*, she says. *You can have it when we get to Bremen.*

Mutti, he says, I am not going to Bremen.

I cannot give it to you now, she says. *You will give it to the girls.*

The girls have gone, Mutti. The girls have gone with Papa. I never see them.

Wolfschen, Wolfschen, come along. We must not miss the train.

She has been dead more than twenty years, and she can still do this to him. He grabs her arm. The box teeters, falls to the floor. He picks it up but he does not look inside. *It will be all right*, he says. The bowl was wrapped in all that silk. It will almost certainly be fine. He will deliver the parcel to Dr. Waldmann, and in all probability Waldmann will not unwrap it either, it is far too precious. The bowl may not have been seen by anyone for generations. If it is broken, that could have happened long ago.

All night Wolf dreams and tosses, wakes and tosses. He dreams of things he finds and then misplaces — his car keys, a certain litho by Chagall.

Love. A word so overworked, but there you are. Everything in Wolf's life was abruptly peeled away, he was not even allowed the option to be loyal, he was left with only fear. And then this past week at Playa de Coco he was given the chance to balance one final beautiful equation. And precisely from the knowledge of his weakness came the key to the riddle of this gift.

For five days he went with Manuel to the islands. They walked the deserted beaches, they swam naked in the sea, they lay upon the sand and read those stories. And the tension of this, the sublime difficulty, coursed through Wolf like a purifying fire.

For five days he lay upon the sand and watched the glassy warm green waves come rolling in, the flights of pelicans go by, the shape of Manuel's brown body striding into the surf, the drops of water flashing from the wild copper curls. This was a scene from Eden, a scene from paradise. With this vision clear inside, Wolf would be able to go on. He would treat Manuel chastely, as a father does a son; he would protect him, educate him, see that the boy received all that was his due. The thought occurred, too — in a country where religion so interweaves with everything — that God might look with interest on one who would accept the challenge of such a plan.

"But what has happened, Manuel?"

The boy steered the course out to the island. He beached the boat. His face was swollen, one eye was black, his shoulder and arm were badly bruised.

"Manuel, Manuel — you have to tell me!"

"It is nothing, *señor*. I fell."

"A fall would not do *that*."

"It is nothing, *señor*. My father was drunk."

"And he hit you? But this is dreadful. No, no — I have to know."

"He found the money that you give. He say bad things. So I must not come with you again. It is not safe for you. And tonight we must bring the boat right to the dock of the hotel. Otherwise he might be waiting on the beach, and I think he will kill you."

Wolf said, "Now come on, Manuel — don't be silly." But he was thinking, *Oh my God, I have been very stupid. I have*

been good-hearted and therefore careless. It should have been obvi-
ous that my good intentions would be misconstrued.

He was thinking how he did not, as it turned out, want
scandal. Nor did he wish to die in some quick useless way. Of
course he also felt outrage that the boy had been exposed to
violence, and because of him. Then he saw that the boy was
shaking, crying. "It is okay," Wolf said. He put a hand on the
boy's slim arm. "Listen...," he said.

"Oh, but *señor* — he is right. My father is a pig, but he is
right. I have not done anything bad, but I know how I am."

In a quiet flip, the world turned over. Wolf did not know
how it happened, but the boy was in his arms. Wolf had been
very good, he had exerted superhuman effort, yet now the
boy was weeping, shaking in his arms. "I want to be with
you, *señor*. I am bad, and I am afraid of what will happen if I
stay here. Please take care of me, *señor*. I know how I am."

Wolf awakes to a ribbon of sound. The song of one particular
bird has been winding through the last segment of his dreams,
looping and repeating in a long bright strand, like the satin
ribbon his sisters used to wear in their hair. The sun has not
yet risen. The jungled hills are waiting to be filled with colour. A fresh wind blows from the grey reclaiming depths of
the sea. He rises, puts on just his bathing suit and sandals. He
starts down the steep path to the shore. Birds dart through
the bushes. He spies a little bird the colour of a ruby, shining
even in the soft grey light. He thinks this is the colour of the
ribbon in his dreams.

Waves pound and flatten and withdraw, leaving white
spume upon the crescent beaches. Wolf follows one long
sandy curve, crosses a tongue of forest, emerges and walks
along the shore again. When the sun hits he kicks off his
sandals, wades into the water. The waves take hold immediately. He lets them carry him out until the bright tile roofs of
the hotel have merged into the green glitter of the jungle
rolling upward. He pictures a Spanish vessel wallowing here,
Vásquez de Coronado looking back and with a rush of glory
observing a tower of smoke raised to the sky. The waves pull

Wolf out in a pillowy swell. He is bobbing like a cork. Easy. He could drift all the way to China, or with a gulp he could be gone.

Yes, he is nothing but a dot on that widening salty landscape, if you looked down from the sky. Not a bad person, not a good person. It all cancels out. But in truth I've led a bad life, he is thinking now. I have fled every difficulty, I have refused to stand up for anything. *And that doesn't look as if it's going to change.* He has to laugh. He watches the shore recede. *Just let go.*

Ah, but here is something — here is an excellent thought. He is getting giddy, perhaps. Lack of food; he hasn't eaten, after all, for almost twenty-four hours. Lack of food, too much sun. He finds himself pondering an idea almost with amusement at the reach of his own folly — at the lengths he's prepared to go to make himself look good — still he is taking it seriously, as well. Suppose that by offering himself to the dark green stony depths, any harm he has done the boy could be expunged.

Then he gets a shiver up the inside of his legs — he gets a feeling of what might be circling under him. He begins to flail towards the shore. What was that flash of understanding? The waves are enormous, now that he decides to fight them. The swells come at him like solid little mountains, and he is weighted as in dreams, with those shadows circling below. And look at him crawling from nothing to nothing. *Abject little worm*, he calls himself. *Coward, fool.*

At last a wave dumps him among the sea-wrack. He could be the first person in the world, half man, half fish — so alone as he creeps out onto the sand, burrows into a warm hollow, stares up at the hard arc of blue. The question he asks could be the first question ever breathed.

In answer, laughter is what he hears. The sound he has imagined all his life, the hidden mirth, made real finally. In this deserted space, in answer to his prayers, he is hearing the laughter of the spheres.

Well, not exactly. For lumbering in his direction along the beach is that couple from the hotel, the big ones — the woman's shrill and merry voice is what he has been hearing, pitted against the roar of the waves.

Quickly, Wolf slides into a hollow among the roots of a driftwood tree. The man has rolled his flapping linen trousers. He is struggling to control a crushed straw hat that is lifting in the breeze. Good heavens, and the woman has taken her clothes off. She is holding her flowered garment in her hand, she is waving it around. She is wearing not one thing. She begins to dance, as she approaches the hollow where Wolf is hiding. She leaps and whirls, and her flesh flies in orbits of its own. "Oh God, oh God, it is wonderful!" she cries. Her eyes are closed. She gives herself to the rhythm of her flesh. She does not see her husband's face. But Wolf does.

Wolf sees the woman's dancing flesh, and he sees the husband's face, and filmed over this he sees a certainty. Things slide out, alive and wild, and you don't know why but you have to crush them. She was beautiful once, and she danced this way for someone else — and nothing vanishes, nothing is ever done with between people, it all lives in the pit of the stomach. *Cut it out*, her husband now will say, *what if someone comes along? Put your robe on for heaven's sake. You look absurd.* Wolf waits to see everything dim.

"Beautiful," the man says. "My love, you are a vision to behold." And this bright lie skitters, refracts and glitters, bursts in blinding light upon the sea.

It was a gruelling climb back to the hotel, for by then the sun was high. All the way up the steep and rocky path — the so-called shortcut — Wolf was making plans. He would pack his bags the moment he got back to his room. He would check out, get out of there immediately. Easter Sunday was a big occasion at the hotel, as he remembered from a previous visit. Many of the wealthy from the uplands, who were down staying at their houses by the sea for Holy Week, made a habit of going to El Más Hermoso for lunch on that day. Maddy always made a special effort. The tables were decorated with little baskets of painted eggs, chocolate rabbits, acid-coloured candies, nestled in shredded cellophane. Sometimes *The Messiah* was playing in the background. Well, he would give that a miss. Without Maddy it was likely to be complete confusion anyway; and even less than yesterday did he want to see Irene. Those gimlet eyes.

Wolf was completely done in when he reached his room. He thought he might be about to have a stroke. He stood underneath a cold shower, trying to figure out his next moves. He would drive to San José and stay at a small hotel he had seen there, not the sort of place where anyone would think to look for him. As soon as he could get a flight, he'd head off to...somewhere. He would work out the fine points on the drive. It was going to be a nuisance not to have ready money, but surely he could use his credit card. He didn't want to hang around till the banks opened, Tuesday probably.

When he stepped out of the shower, he almost slipped and fell. *I feel faint*, he said. He would have to eat. He wished he could phone for room service, but there were no phones in the cabanas. He would have to go to the main building to place his order, no matter what. While he was there he would let them know he was leaving, so they could prepare the bill.

He changed into khaki shorts for driving, and a bright red tank top. As an afterthought, he slung a silky Italian sweater around his shoulders, to add what he hoped was an air of nonchalance. Though with luck he could complete the whole transaction without running into Irene, or even Nelson. With luck, Corazón would be behind the desk at this hour.

He had just gone up the steps into the lobby when Nelson came swishing through the beaded curtain from the dining terrace, moving uncharacteristically fast. Had Wolf surprised a peculiar look on the fellow's face? Something furtive but delighted? Nelson was balancing a tray that held a chocolate milkshake and a large grilled T-bone, two items Wolf had never seen on the menu.

Wolf stopped by the glass case where the jade fetishes had lain. A small piece of modern sculpture had taken the place of the jade, a piece by Zúñiga, perhaps: a broad-hipped kneeling woman holding a baby in her arms.

Nelson's trajectory took him towards a bookcase on the far side of the room, where a few English-language volumes were kept — some mysteries, romances. When he turned back, with a volume in the hand that wasn't balancing the tray, he took note of Wolf for the first time. "Something wrong, man?" he said.

"No no. Not at all. I am merely curious about this piece of sculpture. When was it put here, do you know?"

Nelson shrugged. "It has been in that case as long as I worked here, for sure."

Wolf did not know what to say to this. *It's nothing to me. I'm leaving anyway.*

"It's quite remarkable."

Nelson shrugged again, then started on his way.

"Oh, Nelson," Wolf called after him. "I would like some lunch, in my room. Could you bring me over a club sandwich and some soda?"

"No problem. I'll bring it right away." Which meant, Wolf thought, that he ought to be able to eat in at most an hour. Well, he would take a nap while he was waiting; he was feeling rather dizzy again.

"Thank you very much. I hate to trouble you. You look as if you've got a lot on your plate today."

Nelson gave him an unexpected grin, and raised his eyebrows as if to say, *You don't know the half of it.* "Oh, hey, Mr. Lazarus — I almost forgot. There is a message for you in your box. Would you mind?" He made a juggling motion to indicate how full his hands were. "We are short-staffed today — Corazón is helping in the kitchen, and I am supposed to be keeping an eye on the desk, but I'd better get on out there with these."

"No of course," Wolf said. "I will get it. But when you have a moment...."

Nelson swished out through the beaded curtain, without hearing the end of Wolf's request. Anyway, Wolf was feeling more and more peculiar. He had to lean on the desk. Another message for Mr. Lazarus. He could see it waiting there, in one of the wooden pigeonholes on the wall. This did not strike Wolf as amusing any more. He felt he was moving through a dream, everything wavery and changing — a Zúñiga where the axe-gods were supposed to be, and Charles Lazarus butting in again.

This one was not a hotel envelope. Indeed the thick white stationery had a threatening legal look. *I don't need to open this*, Wolf thought. There were people like that; André used to be like that. If a piece of mail had an unpleasant look to it, André simply tucked it away until he felt up to it, or until it melted into the underbrush of other undone things. Nothing drastic had ever seemed to come of that approach. *There could be a lot of better ways of approaching things*, Wolf was thinking, *than I have always used.* Charles Lazarus, for example — he would not feel impelled to rip open an envelope that had such an ominous look.

Dear Mr. Lazarus, the letter read (and the letter itself was on hotel stationery), *This is to remind you that another party has made a booking for cabana 25, beginning tomorrow, Monday. We have appreciated your patronage in the past, and regret that you will not be staying with us again. Yours sincerely, The Management. PS: Checkout time is ten AM.*

Oh that's perfect, Wolf heard himself say. Absolutely Jim Dandy, as that American soldier of his mother's used to say repeatedly. Those voices from the past that kept bursting in! *And who exactly is she, anyway, Wolfschen?* his mother was demanding now, *Just a woman from Vancouver* (for of course the letter was Irene's work), *Wolf, you must keep in mind that we come from a very aristocratic family. We do not allow ourselves to be spoken to this way.*

Yes Mutti yes, he said, as so often in the past. *Please do not upset yourself.*

Still, what did he care? Certainly he had booked the cabana for a week, but he had decided he was leaving anyway. *Her insults will roll off my water like a duck,* he said — one of the turns of phrase his mother had been taken with, when she first arrived in Canada.

But I will show her a thing or two. If Irene thought that note was going to get rid of him today — or even make him stick to his room — she was mistaken. *Because now I've got my gander up,* he said. (Another of his mother's choice turns of phrase.) He straightened his back, rearranged the silk sweater around his shoulders, pushed through the beaded curtain, went up to the bar. "Would you please tell Nelson that I have changed my mind about my order," he told the boy, Rodrigo. "I am going to spend the afternoon by the pool. I would like my lunch down there."

So now Wolf emerges once again into this setting that is close to paradise — the brilliant water, the flowers, the broad-leafed shimmering trees. The scene hits him with particular force, perhaps because of the state he is in. He could weep, all at once, for the beauty of the world.

Then he sees something that knocks his breath away. He cannot believe his eyes. On the far side of the pool, in a reclining lounger that Wolf has never seen before — one that has an awning attached to it, fringed and tasselled like the shade of an oriental palanquin — is Maddy Wilkes. She is wearing large dark glasses of the sort that film stars used to wear, and a red linen dress and gold earrings the size of jarlids. And it is to Maddy that Nelson has been rushing with the steak and the milkshake. All attentive, he has pulled a small table close beside her, set down the book and the tray. Wolf is just in time to see her wave him away.

"Oh hi, hello...!" she calls out, while Wolf is trying to decide if he is seeing things. "I've missed you this morning." As if it were the most natural thing in the world for her to be there at all, let alone lying by the pool, which is something she has rarely done before. "Come on over!" she calls.

"Don't look so surprised, dear," she says, when he has pulled up a chair. "Yes, so here I am!" But now that he is close, he sees that her face is puffy. Behind the glasses, it could be that she is badly bruised around the eyes.

She leans forward, beckons him closer. She smells of some expensive perfume that has gone off, an acrid puzzling smell. "Wolf, she was magnificent!"

"Irene?"

"Yes, of course. She's like nobody else, Wolf. She's like ...destiny. Can you imagine what that means to me?"

"Yes, I believe I can...." And he can, that is the trouble. He remembers exactly how it feels when the course of your existence is taken from your hands.

"As soon as she figured out I'd gone, she didn't mess around at all. She'd driven all the way from Quetal, but she got right back in the Land Rover and took off after me. Heavens, she must have gone like a bat out of hell, because I'd hardly even checked in...."

"How did she know where you were?"

"Oh well, there's a place we always stay in San José. I thought I'd be okay there for just one night, but I underestimated her. I'd barely finished bathing and changing when there was this terrific hammering at the door. Of course I didn't open it. So she got the manager, but he didn't have an extra key, so she *made him take the door right off the hinges!* It was terrifying, I even thought of climbing out the window, but it was thrilling too! She was like the wrath of God or something, the way she burst into that room."

"*Ja*...Maddy...that's wonderful," he said. "But, what...?" He feels his hands go to his face.

"Oh yes, that's rather awful, isn't it? I went off the road on the way up — slammed myself right against the windshield. But then I managed to back and fill till I got the Jeep out of the ditch, and I just carried on. Lord, I think I went kind of nuts yesterday. But here I am, Wolf! Right back where I started." She laughs gaily. "But with an understanding of how foolish I was. I know why I came here in the first place — somehow I'd forgotten that. I know how she needs me. And," Maddy giggles, "she says she is going to treat me like the Queen of Sheba from now on." Then this bright expression glazes over. A shadow falls across Wolf's chair, from behind.

"Well, Mr. Lazarus!"

Wolf springs to his feet. "Forgive me, Irene. Have I taken your seat?"

"I fear you have."

She sits down. Wolf dithers for a moment. Nelson arrives, carrying Wolf's lunch, amazingly prompt. "Nelson, Mr. Lazarus is sitting over there," Irene says, gesturing at a chair across the pool.

Why should he lower himself to care whether he made a graceful exit, or stumbled away? Look at the two of them with their heads together: Irene handing Maddy first her drink, then her plate, her knife and fork, flipping open the napkin. How I pity them, Wolf thinks, to his surprise. Yet he suspects envy is what he means. Isn't it better to be locked together in any sort of hell than to be free and rolling empty around the world? But are they talking about him? They must be. Wolf is the villain, is that it? He lent money to a lady in distress.

Which he will never get back. No matter what he does. That will be the second half of Irene's joke — that he will not have the nerve even to demand that his loan be used to cover his bill. She knows he will never make a fuss. She doesn't know what his problem is, but she knows that Mr. Lazarus is on the run. *We have appreciated your patronage, and regret that you will not be staying with us again.*

Well, I have had enough of this, Wolf thinks. *They believe they can make fun of me, but I will not be bullied into staying here and taking anything the two of them dish out. I will leave, the moment I have finished my lunch.* If he suspects a certain contradiction of purpose over the last few minutes, it's a bit hazy. But now he cannot eat his sandwich. He should have ordered yogurt, something slippery and calm. The layers of toast, the prickly edges of bacon — the pickle! — there is no way he is going to get that down.

And they are looking at him again, from across the pool. And even more unsettling, that man Wolf last saw at breakfast yesterday, that darkish maybe German-looking man, *with a sneaky lemur face,* has pulled up a chair beside Irene.

This is too exhausting. Wolf pictures a ping-pong ball flipping back and forth as fits of dudgeon slap him this way and that. But the truth is, he simply does not have the energy to get up and go anywhere just now. *Well, and anyway,* he thinks — after picking the turkey out of his sandwich and managing to eat a bit of that, at least — *if she thought I was going to slink away, she is quite mistaken. Her mean-spirited message has had quite the opposite effect.* He decides to take this line and stick to it. Even though a feeling is growing on him that everybody here knows something that he doesn't. Nelson, for example;

what is going on with Nelson? So attentive. "You don't like your sandwich, Mr. Lazarus? Can I bring you something else? Some soda? Sure; *sin hielo, claro!* — don't you worry Mr. Lazarus, it's on its way."

Others — passing bathers, waiters too — are carefully hiding their smiles; and though this has always been the case, he feels it more sharply this afternoon. He has never fitted anywhere. *All you sleek people,* he wants to shout, *you are looking at a man who did not fit in even with the alcoholics, when he joined AA.* The memory, one of the most awful moments of his life, sets off the siren in his head. He shrinks in his chair. When you have been sober for a year, they bake you a cake, and they call it your birthday, and you are supposed to stand up and make a speech, the worse the better — tell how you hit bottom, describe the piece of hell you wallowed in before you allowed the Higher Power to turn your life around. And he fell for that. Carried away by the drama of his own story, he described how he had woken up naked, battered, on the edge of Golden Gate Park, near the windmill. Nearly dead, but not quite. Something warm was lying near. A large black dog. Though later it was gone. He did not think it was a dream.

All those eyes. Perhaps a hundred people staring. He left the stage and left the hall, and never went back to those meetings again.

And tomorrow he is leaving El Más Hermoso, and he is going somewhere else — and somewhere after that — and he will keep moving the way a shark must, for he does not have the courage for the other thing. But he will not feel the touch of another person, ever. He will not allow himself a situation where he might hurt yet another human being.

The poolside music is more upbeat this afternoon. There has been a little jazz, a little salsa — and now, to Wolf Lehmann's dismay, they are playing the whole of *Jesus Christ Superstar*.

He has found himself a lounge-bed in the shade of a palm-thatched umbrella, and he refuses to give it up, even to go in and get something to read. He holds his ground. He tries to sleep, but fails. This is not a restful place today. Though no small children are allowed, slim brown teenagers are throwing one another in the water, and their parents are calling out from group to group, and a tense electric buzz vibrates over everything — the crickets in the trees. The first time Wolf was here, he saw one of those crickets. It was about the size of a sea-horse, and it had the same fixed smile. Come to think of it, it had the smile of the fat lady.

Oh the fat lady, the fat lady. She does not have much to sing about after all. The truth is, she has let Wolf down.

He thought he had witnessed a moment of epiphany, down there on the beach. Yet where is the husband now? Why is the wife back on her own? How hard to be the mate of a purveyor of moral uplift! "Oh, I live for others," people like that say. Absolutely. She swallows them whole. *A woman of voracious appetite and food alone won't do it.* Avid, the way she leans forward as she sketches, feeding on the faces and the gestures of the unwary as they play. She wears reflecting glasses today, so her victims will not know. She misses not one thing, not the Danes floating in dejected circles on their matching air mattresses, not the man from Thunder Bay frog-kicking with a tray for his cigarettes and beer, not the appalling antics of the young, hitting the water like cannonballs. She smiles and smiles. *Just once, I would dearly love to see that smile gone from her face*, Wolf says.

And now, once more, she turns her chair in Wolf's direction. He feels her tracing the outlines of his face, capturing, without exaggeration, its vapid quality, his fear of everything. And he has had it with her. He is sick of being made a fool of by every person in the world. He will show her how he feels.

He sits up and looks at her. And she, the bitch, takes off her glasses, waves.

"You've caught me," she calls across, as blithely as can be. "So now I owe you something. Come — join me for a drink!"

Everyone is staring. What can Wolf do? He is the prisoner of decency.

"The thing is," she says as he approaches, "you look so nice. I just couldn't resist you." She laughs. "And of course you sit so still. But whenever I first saw you I said, *Now I must draw* him."

"Nice."

"A dirty word? Well, of course extremely interesting too." She scans the drawing, then passes him the pad. "I sense you are a very troubled man."

He looks at what she has done and he cannot believe it. This is his face, no doubt about it, yet it is a face so full of character, so full of honourable strife. This preposterous woman, bathed in her husband's lies all her life, is a miracle: one of those rare creatures who see good in everything.

He wants to kneel. In fact he does. He stumbles somehow, bumps the table, knocks the chocolate box containing all her charcoals to the ground. He kneels to gather these, fumbles in the powdery mess of charcoal sticks and bits of chalk and pencil stubs and old rubber bands, and the loudspeakers are rocking out the Resurrection, and tears are streaming down his face.

"Hey," she says, "it's okay. Here." She hands him her sketch-rag. He blows his nose. "I think you should tell me," she says.

"So," she says, "you have done a very bad thing. No matter how it turns out, what you have done is very bad, because the possibility was there. I take it you don't know for sure?"

"Not for sure. I was afraid to have the tests. But how could it be otherwise? Of course once I knew the danger, I promised myself that I'd...."

"Behave?"

The late-afternoon heat has filled up all the spaces on the terrace, and there is not a stir of air. Wolf has moved onto a chair of course; he is no longer on his knees. The heady rush of confession is over. He feels ridiculous and stuck. He would like to run — head down to Panama, Colombia, God knows, buy a boat and smuggle dope — or be back where he was ten minutes ago, juggling guilt, uncertainty.

"Yes, well you have behaved despicably," she is saying. "But you are not a bad man. You just got pushed around, like all the rest of us" — she pats her huge flesh — "by things you don't understand."

"And maybe," she is saying, "not that it would make much of a difference, but have you thought of this? Maybe the boy wasn't all that innocent, you know. Maybe you got taken in by a pretty little tart."

She sits there square as a church. Wolf has offered up his most intimate shame and guilt to her, and she says such an ugly thing — and it is the same thought he has allowed himself from time to time. Oh God, his heart fills with the boy, something he has been holding off. He hates her, hates this. This is worse than anything, if he has exposed himself to someone no better than himself. "Who are you?" he asks, surprising them both. "I mean, your work is extraordinary. How have I missed it? You must be quite well known."

She laughs. "I could have been, perhaps. It's easy to say that, isn't it?"

"But you have such an eye." He has to make this clear. "Believe me, I know about these things."

"You might say my husband is someone. Under a variety of names. I merely type his manuscripts, and answer the mail. He writes novels of" — she grasps her tented bosom, lets go a sound like ripping cloth from between her half-clenched teeth — "historical romance," she says, "if you see what I mean. As for this little passion" — she flicks the pages of her sketchbook — "I only indulge when we're away on holiday."

This little passion.... Wolf sees her dancing on the sand.

She is leaning towards him now, wheezing, giving off a hot camphor smell. She puts a hand not on his knee but on the webbing of his chair. "The thing is," she whispers, "that I know. Believe me. Listen. I know how important it can seem, to seize things. Time passes. And everything one feared is true. The chance never comes again." She flops back in her seat, as if she has handed him a thing of tender beauty which he now must help her hold.

"But of course you'll return," she says. "To Playa de Coco, I mean."

"I can't. Holy mother of God, they'll crucify me."

"I doubt it." She is not smiling any more. "At the very worst you may end up in prison. But if you're rich.... No, you'll go back. You must take him up to San José; you must both of you have tests; and if the worst comes to the worst, at least you can help him. Don't worry" — she pats his chair again — "you won't have to live and die a lonely fugitive. You'll be able to pay."

She sits and blinks in the sunlight, for a moment satisfied. Wolf sees what a joke this is. He is a small man, he is no one, he is surely insignificant. Yet she will track him to the ends of the earth, she will see that he walks the last mile on his knees, for the lonely wife of a writer of romance has caught the scent of righteousness.

She sits and blinks and feeds on his salvation. The sky turns the colour of fire. The iguana creeps from the shade and starts along the terrace wall, inching forward for no reason anyone can tell.

THE QUEEN OF SAXONY

The Queen of Saxony ran off with her children's music teacher, an Italian who was scarcely older than her eldest child. This happened when my father was a boy. She left behind five sons, crown jewels that dated from the Holy Roman Empire, the pony that pulled the dogcart in which she sometimes let the boys who lived next to the Summer Palace ride — and a husband who, quite soon, would be forced to abdicate. She left behind a country which would shortly disappear. But I doubt if she anticipated that.

Why am I doing this? she may have asked herself. *Shouldn't five sons, a dogcart and those pendants and tiaras — and the cross of Henry the Bear oozing historic light upon the breast of any wearer (me) — shouldn't all that be enough? And this Italian, although his body skin is smoother than the smoothest almond paste, is just another* child. *I'll have to teach him everything, I won't be able to resist, it's in my nature to give orders — and he will grow to hate me, and I'll grow old and fat and more and more addicted to spaghetti.*

Now the King was a charming, kindly man. Perhaps he pinched a chambermaid occasionally, no more. He was plump, with bushy eyebrows and a booming Saxon laugh. And the Queen packed her seven oak-bound trunks, and fled.

How could she do that? How could she do that to her children, to her husband, to the nation? That is what they muttered in the gargoyled, corniced, fluted streets of Dresden, in the courtyard of the Zwinger Palace, in the Hofkirche, beneath the rococo vaults of the cathedral, along the cobbled alleys of that extraordinary city built to glorify the infrangible Saxon spirit and last a thousand years.

Of course we know similar tales. Our view may be milder; scandal is hardly an issue any more and, as for people getting hurt, it's an equation. Things happen. Someone is always in the line of fire. Still, we collect these stories. And if we take them out from time to time and polish them, the way our grandmothers buffed up Apostle spoons, it could be to get a shiver of something that, in another age, was looked for in Salvation. Life after Reality, you might say.

I wish I knew what happened to the Queen of Saxony. But then, I also wish I knew what happened to Adele. People get lost. Even quite important people get lost. With Adele, it was borderline.

I must confess I never liked Adele much. She was always so well dressed; and she talked so well, and knew so much, and had a disarming trivial streak — yet there was something about her that felt as if it could be catching, some deep unease. So I suspect nothing happened to her. She was certainly not brave. I expect that, after that night, she just went on and on, in the same way.

I will tell you what I do know of her story. And I will try to be unbiased. I must ask you to put yourself in Adele's place, though, or it all may look smaller than a gnat's ear, as Adele's mother used to say. Adele's mother was not given to people thinking about themselves. One accepted the life God gave one and just got on with things, that was Adele's mother's point of view — and Adele did more or less that all those years on the knife-edge of a marriage that was the envy of almost everyone she knew.

I will call this story "Accident." And I should add that it took place a number of years ago.

You have just been hit by a bus, but you certainly don't show it. You are Adele, of course; you are the wife of the Dean of Latin American Studies, and your husband is hosting this affair in honour of an extremely elevated personage who has flown in from Ottawa. The moment has arrived, though, for you to ease them both away for one of those elegant small suppers you are known for, which make the rest of us despair. A few selected guests will sip Brunello in your Mexican-tiled kitchen, and clever talk will fly around while you grill the lamb, braise the sorrel, toss a salad of fresh greens. Later I expect you will whip up one of your famous Camembert soufflés. This is quintessential Adele — the woman who can steer an important evening (for this could nail down a quasi-diplomatic posting for your husband) between the shoals of too much wit and heavy-duty political discussion while grilling lamb and producing a perfect golden puffed soufflé. Also you yourself are no small thing in academic circles, though in an area so rarefied that there are maybe twenty people in the world you can really talk to, and in your present state of mild concussion you have lost the point. Still, look at the way you hold yourself. Look at the way you take your husband's arm as you leave this panelled room. Your fingers rest lightly on grey flannel that has the merest stripe of puce, a stripe so fine you'd have to know him awfully well to notice it at all.

You kiss the wife of the Chancellor on the cheek, give a steady hand to the head of your department, praise Poppy Melville on her dress though she has always hated you. "Golly," you say, "you really are so clever; I wish *I* could sew." A thin glaze is all that holds your parts together. You are careful of the way you tilt your chin. You are a forty-three-year-old woman wearing flat bronze shoes and bronze tights and a cashmere dress not much longer than a shirt — the most extreme form of self-expression (leaving aside for the moment the focus of your recent academic writing) your severest critic could accuse you of. You are Adele and you have travelled around the world, to spots of danger, too — yet when the moment came for you to bite the dust, it was in Vancouver British Columbia Canada, at a faculty club affair.

Why not last winter in the Boulevard St. Michel, say? Out of that I could produce a far more likely scene.

See how the steam is condensing on the windows of a glassed-in sidewalk café. You are drinking a *grand crème* taking your chances with the terror that has made Paris quieter this year. You are writing postcards to your children, two of them at home still, the others feigning independence in countries you have visited or intend to visit soon. The air is thick with Gauloise smoke, and across from you is a man you know so well that whenever a woman enters and his eyes twitch up from the *Herald Tribune*, twitch and linger (and as this process continues you diminish; your shoes, although you bought them yesterday, become Canadian and dull), the discomfort you feel is a familiar one, a pain you have adjusted to and readjusted to, and are adjusting to again. You say to yourself, so what? You say to yourself, when I get back home my paper on *Prosas Profanas* will be causing a flurry, a scandal even, in the tiny tiny circle where such things are life and death. And anyway in a minute I am going to go out and buy myself some little self-indulgent thing. Maybe a belt like the one on that slim dark woman by the bar, dressed in urban-terror chic — the one his eyes have steadfastly removed the clothes from, piece by dangerous piece: a black leather belt trimmed with what appears to be a row of submachine-gun bullets. Yes.

Things are good. You know what the rest of your life will be like, you know that if you are very lucky it will always be like this: a thin warm jelly studded with small sharp objects through which you will swim, having long ago learned to breathe below the surface—

"*Hey,*" a young man says, who has barged across the floor of the Faculty Club, "*hey I find you very....*"

— and then the Paris café is ripped apart by a bomb blast. There are bodies all over the place, bodies and pieces of bodies. Your husband and even your children in those far-off countries are torn into colourful flat fragments like bits of a cartoon. And in the moment of the explosion you have not only been blown clear, you have become the woman in the black machine-gun belt. You step daintily through the rubble, holding your chin at a certain angle. "Goodbye dear," you say again to Poppy Melville before you air-kiss her husband, a renowned expert on the love life of the paramecium, "*Adios.*"

Or it could be Nicaragua. Yes, that is closer to the core.

It is the dry season, and it is still the era of the Sandinistas. It is the season when guerrilla forces everywhere are on the move. You have driven in from the south, along a road that, as you approached the border, wound through straw-coloured hills, groves of flame-trees. You crossed the border at Peñas Blancas. Your vehicle was fumigated twice. You refused the air-conditioned car that was offered by the embassy, not wanting to look too much like honchos, and now you are hurtling from bump to bump in a jeep driven by Roberto, a Costa Rican who, his national pride at stake, is driving even more badly than the Nicaraguans — that is to say, like a man with an urgent need to end things here and now. And this is good. This is how things ought to be. You are passing the lake where Somosa threw the bodies. You are passing the hills where the Contras stop the northward-spreading cancer by blowing up the schools. It is good to feel pared down; to be aware, right from the start, that in this country one is always nose to nose with death. Your aim is to see things as they are.

So you are weaving between bumps, crashing through potholes, flying over bridges guarded by young boys with submachine-guns; and the air smells first of Flit and then, pervasively, of the Givenchy perfume that has broken in your bag. And on the right, beyond the golden stubble-covered fields, the lake rises and falls, and in the lake there are volcanoes and they also rise and fall, rise and fall and lurch. And on the road, army trucks roar past, even though Roberto will not pull over they roar past, filled with boys and girls in khaki. And in the back of that one — there — is a tall girl with a face from before the Spanish conquest, the face of an idol from Zapetera, with long black hair that coils and uncoils in the wind; and beneath the khaki she is huge with child. And as for the man in the back seat beside you, in his bush-shirt with the many many pockets, he says, "Oh!" — that's all.

And from the hollow of that little word acres of swampland roll out for just a moment, and then furl up again into something smaller than anything anyone would care to think about, and he passes you the *agua minerale* and you take a drink.

And then the jeep pulls out to repass the army truck, and you are facing a red-and-blue painted bus so jammed with people that they are hanging on the sides — and the roof is piled with crates of chickens, and behind the chickens is the entire Rivas youth club baseball team....

"*Hey,*" the young man says, over the hum of cocktail talk, "*I find you very —*"

WHAM.

So prosaic. Yes, I am going to have to take you back to that room where a woman called Adele — dressed but not too much so, a little high but in control — has been carrying on a completely respectable conversation in the safest place in the world.

...*fascinating to converse with,* she felt sure he was about to say, this unlikely boy, some travelling post-grad Fellow who had the size and texture of a woolly mammoth, and a rampaging style. He had already towed her, laughing, out of breath, through half a dozen disciplines, scattering the fences, tearing up the wire. Then he landed on the area she knew best, and he paused and listened to her. He caught her ideas and tossed them around so all the facets struck the light, and flipped them back with variations, and she felt supple as a circus person, flushed and young.

Or...*expressive when you talk in Spanish; and your voice is just right for Darío, have you been an actress?* Something like that, he would say. Then, *Olímpico pájaro, herido de amor,* he would echo, this boy who was young enough to be one of her own sons. He was only a year or so older than Michael. She felt a lid slide from a space inside her, a sort of trap. She had raised five children, yet it seemed those years of riches had collapsed into a slim envelope which she wore pinned above her heart, afraid to open it. Her sons were far away, and her eldest had somehow been transformed into a complicated handsome stranger with a profile like an arrow, tense and quivering. Yet now she remembered, exactly, painfully, the hollow in the nape of his neck when he was only three, also the smell of him. She remembered lifting him on one particular day, her hands beneath his armpits. He was wearing a red-and-green-striped T-shirt. His small body pulsed with a smell that was like breathing life itself, hot and grotty and intense, sweet as hay — and she remembered the sharp little angles of his ribs. What had been the point of all that, then? If she had not, unwittingly and step by step, committed the folly of giving those boys confidence and independence, pointing out the breadth and beauty of the world to them, perhaps she would not now be all at once confused. She had almost reached out to touch this other boy, this grown one, this man. It had seemed the most natural thing in the world to circle that gruff space at the base of his pulled-back hair, to receive the texture, the smell upon her fingers. A sick longing for something absolutely lost rushed through her and away before she had a chance to trace it.

Anyway, he did not in any way resemble a child of hers. He was all bulk, but with nice details — the small blue stone that twinkled in one ear, the way the rough-sheared curls of face and head frizzed out into a ponytail tied with Christmas string. And the hairy surface seemed extensive; dark whorls and counter-whorls could be conjectured from the neckline of the grey mechanic's overall he wore. If all those snaps should pop, one might find a coarsely curling surface, warm and somewhat prickly, like a fireside rug.

Olímpico pájaro..., she blithely had been quoting. Olympian bird, swollen with love. Swollen. This from her controversial translation. And he had seen immediately how "wounded" wouldn't do, how that fainting *fin-de-siècle* transfer into English of the lines from "Leda" did not convey the revolutionary shock of Darío at all. Swollen with love, she'd said. She could say anything she wanted. "Adele is being wicked again" was the most anyone might dare; "Look at her being wicked again, in her safe pathetic way."

"I find you very..." — *helpful* — *the things you've told me about how to get around in Nicaragua...!* Yes of course. For this boy was heading down there to do research for his book. She could hear his next words — *and you say your daughter is married, more or less, to a member of the government down there? The Minister of Culture is your very close friend? Say, I wonder....* Yes, she could help him. She could help him a whole lot.

"I find you very attractive." The words cut right across her half-completed sentence.

And that was *all?*

Wait — think of the expression on his face. So calm and purposeful.

Oh really; oh for heaven's *sake.*

It can't be helped. At the heart of any story such as this there is a moment like the centre of a chocolate cream. Intelligent people wince, climb into their Jeep Cherokees, head for exercise class. Adele knows this too. Adele knows that everyone she knows would close the book at this point.

They would sneak back later, all the same. They would creep back with their plain brown wrappers and their flashlights just because of who she is, just because they would love to see her make a fool of herself for once, just because they had to know what happened, plain self-admitted prurience.

What happened indeed? What happened, Adele? *How could you?*

She is looking in the mirror now, late at night, having climbed out of bed wearing a flannel nightgown printed with small orange flowers. There is a film over the room behind her — the lace curtains sewn from Chinese tablecloths, the framed cartoons, the ferns in hanging baskets made one summer at a commune in the Kootenays, the bright red bath they bought when they got back, the matching toilet and the bidet used for washing pantihose. The whole room is filmed and sticky with years. Against it she stands out sharply, in a flare of absurdity.

Well, she cracked open like a walnut, pieces scattered on the floor. "Oh!" she said. And then she laughed. "That's nice. I think that's very nice." So gauche, her limbs flying out at all angles. As if she'd never had a compliment before.

If she could go over it again it would be different. "I thought you were about to say 'intelligent,'" she'd say. "That's a far better line. There is a story by Cheever, do you know it? A man falls for an extremely beautiful girl who is just a little dim? He finally comes to understand that the way to get her into bed is to ignore her beauty and go on and on about her brain...?"

(Oh god, not bed — thank the lord she didn't say that!)

Adele does go over it again. She goes over it and over it — one smallish woman in a flannel nightgown, with a fate no different than the fate of any grand imperious nation: condemned to relive the past, relive it and relive it, learning very little, nothing in fact.

"That's nice...." Looking first at the floor and then across the room at that dress of Poppy Melville's, a perfect academic-wife dress, printed acetate that looks a bit like tweed — and there go Poppy's teeth, shooting forward in her famous smile, the terror of every new man on the faculty.... Yes, the woman who had just been blown sky-high, thinking that.

And this gets worse and worse.

For now it was clear that he had been taken horribly aback by Adele's reaction. His face was being consumed by a slow rush of flame. A boy far from home, singed to a crisp, it was hardly fair; and so young he couldn't even hide the pity he felt.

His eyes, though. Remember his eyes. They did not seem to share that alarmed point of view. He looked down at the floor, where his feet were doing a shuffle, then back up at her. *That's just fine*, his eyes conveyed — *Adele, relax, it's all okay; I meant what I said.* His eyes were the absolute clear startling blue of mountain pools, and she was teetering on a high place in the grip of vertigo. An electric current was racing from the soles of her feet right up the insides of her legs, and at the crucial moment she mistook this for a surge of inspiration. Well, she thought, at least I can teach him how a grown woman handles things.

"I think you are blushing," she said.

He mistook what she had said, in the din of the crowd. "That's okay," he said. "It suits you. Besides, I'm blushing too."

Oh hopeless, hopeless, and he was so pleased with this gift of skewed gallantry. And she would have to set him straight. She could not stand imprecision, lack of order, loose ends of any sort. Besides, did she ever blush? Excuse me, but I said that *you* are blushing, she would have to say. She was doing a free-fall, though. She was plunging through space and she was crooning as she fell, and far below she saw a shining city built of exactly such silly gilded arcs of mis-communication, the cardboard castles, the gorgeous leaning towers, and she was quite happy spiralling down; it was an intrusion that more words were now required. Anyway every clever thought had fled, leaving just one sentence, so inap-propriate and simple: COME ON THEN, LET'S GET OUT OF HERE...!

She glanced around at all the people using words accept-ably. Of course her husband. Look at him fanning out the right phrase every time, with the flair of *cuisine minceur*, de-lighting the wife of the Chancellor, training his quizzical at-tention upon the comely graduate student (comely and of course brilliant, also poleaxed by his charm, just as Adele herself had been when he had called her in to talk about her very first term paper) whose turn it was to be a shadow in the landscape round him for a month or so. His way at moments like this was to draw you out and draw you out, then lance in with a response that turned common thought upon its head. Adele could hear the laughter. He had done it again. And no one would ever accuse him of making a display, in public, out of keeping with his role; and Adele was yoked to him, and by the same token she would never let him go. He was nimble, exceptional. She was so accustomed now to the taste of distrust.

Still, if she made one move she could break out, right now, over bodies that crumpled up like eggshells, wading through stunned glances, dropped teeth, everything. And so quick. So complete. A complete redefinition, think of that.

Well...," she was saying, at that same time, "it's been...! Hasn't it?" And she was thrusting out her hand to that young man. She was flashing a completely stupid smile. She was turning away, not in control of this at all, carrying the impression that the two halves of his face had shifted, as if abruptly snipped apart. She was crossing the room, she was gathering up her husband, she was making her way out quite steadily, sucking in her stomach, tilting up her chin.

But everything is cracked and broken anyway. Even though she is locked, virtuous, in her own silent bathroom, everything is cracked and broken, none of the edges line up, probably they never lined up. And her bones ache. Something absolutely vital has been injected, then withdrawn.

She should have paid attention to lessons of geography. The voices of her two daughters, just along the hall, whisper in sleep like waves uncurling on a shore where she has lived, but very long ago. She feels their dreaming lap around her and she is a rope in those dreams, trying to tie the waves to the sand; she is a thin-twigged lashing tree with arms that block the sun, with roots that tie everything to yesterday — and her leaves turn yellow and fall upon the water and drift away.

But you do not get second chances in this life. That is one thing Adele has told others, frequently. It is possible that she has lived her whole life second-hand — that awful thought is settling around her like cement — but she has given good advice, sustaining herself by wise wise words; and still she is without the courage or the grace to swallow them.

Once she sat through a long night of withdrawal with an alcoholic friend. It was terrible. The woman reeked, she flailed and twitched, she cried out that her brain was dead. The terror she conveyed was the worst thing — the sense of doom that seeped from all the corners of the room. Next day that friend did the obvious sensible thing, and crawled out to buy another week's supply of gin.

But for the likes of you, Adele, there are no second chances.

That lovely man will go on, far away. You will not get in touch with him tomorrow, on the pretext of helping to plan his trip. That is the sort of thing other people do. You will not arrange an innocent lunch at some out-of-the-way place, say the Teahouse in the park. (So there is no point giving thought to what to wear.) You will not provide him with a letter to the Minister of Culture. You will not write ahead to make it possible, that scheme he has to travel the old trade route from the lake down to the Mosquito coast, along the San Juan River, through the border territory that is still a covert battle zone. And when his plane drones south above the spine of the Americas, above the volcanoes, above the rain-forests where snakes coil within the shadows and yard-wide bats slide down the air, and small transparent frogs, like beads of deadly condensation, gleam in the hollows of the roots of the gigantic trees — and when the lightning flashes and the battlemented clouds flare up against the sky, terrible and luminous as dreams — you will not be in the seat beside him. You will be preparing your lecture on erotic images in symbolist poetry.

She searches out a nail file, she sits on the toilet seat, she begins to file her nails. It is a relief to have something positive to do, to take her mind off the crumbling all around. Her hands are thin and birdlike, like her face, and they have been skilled, they always have been best, at simply holding on.

She finds herself thinking of her mother's hands. What a thing at a time like this, your mother's hands — such beautiful cool hands, smelling of expensive leather, fine-milled soap — hands that knew instinctively the gestures of acceptance or curtailment that would serve. Adele's mother could have married any man, she often said so. She chose the one who showed the most efficiency, the one with the whip-sharp mind. And everything Adele's father forgets these days is chalked up as a victory by Adele's mother in their long silent undercover war.

Ah but Adele, tonight you had an accident, is that it? Things blew apart, though it was just a man telling you that you were attractive, and probably he didn't mean it. That is not the point, you say. Even the man is not the point. Something else has been presented, something swift and clear —

though now it crinkles in your mind and slips away.

For who gave you the thought that your life was yours, anyway? You could take out entire lives — you could wipe out five childhoods with just one whim. A parent must guard the past with every tool available, because look at the mess that could be waiting in the future, not even air to breathe; and don't tell me that's not *your* fault — in fact, hang your head in guilt for a life lived second-hand. And let me add this. If you use that excuse to do some stupid thing now, to shame your husband, he will never forgive. You don't get second chances. You said that — you.

But tonight I had an accident, she says.

All the same, things are settling down. Dawn is spilling through the lace pattern of the curtains, a helpful light the shade of Listerine. Shapes creep back into the corners, shedding camouflage. From her point of vantage on that bright red piece of plumbing, Adele is afforded a clear unclouded vista of who and where she really is. And now I have arrived at the dry season, she says.

She grabs at anything she can, any reviving scrap of foolishness. Her hand closes on something shining in the dust, just a fragment, sharp as glass — but look, it holds reflections. She brings it closer. She sees straw-coloured hills, flame trees. She sees the season she has entered thanks to the merest accident. It is shimmering with heat, dazzling her eyes, everything at flashpoint, gorgeous, lethal, extreme. Now she watches herself step across a chasm. *How could she do that?* And light is wobbling all around the small reflected figure that she sees — perhaps the radiance that pours from any finite thing as it dissolves scandalously, sweetly, into myth.

Acknowledgements

Thanks to Shaena Lambert for all the long talks about writing, and for deep insights into the gap between the thought and the word; to Jamie Evrard for encouraging not just me but many others; to Lorna Schwenk for allowing the butterfly to alight on the branch; to Kathleen Conroy for her keen eye and her friendship; to Eva Stachniak for helpful readings of several of these stories; to John Lambert for perceptive comments; to James and Alexa Lambert for giving me Costa Rica (and correcting my Spanish).

Thanks to my agent Carolyn Swayze for faith and guidance; to Gena Gorrell for resolute, tactful editing.

I am particularly indebted to Charlotte Trende, who so generously shared her memories of a childhood in Berlin — and to Victor Janoff, who read an early draft of the novella and gave me courage to tell Wolf's tale.